Alice brought her g
Cristiano's glitterin
surely not going to g
this…are you?'

A smile that wasn't quite a smile courted the edges of his mouth. 'But of course. It is what Nonna wanted. Who am I to disregard her last wishes?'

Alice frowned so hard she might have frightened off twenty ampoules of Botox. 'What happens if I don't agree?'

'To me?' He gave a careless shrug. 'Nothing—other than losing a few shares in the company, which will pass to a relative if I don't comply with the terms of the will.'

Alice wondered how important those shares were to him. Was his easy-come-easy-go shrug disguising deeper, far more urgent motivations? Enough to marry someone he now hated?

She sent her tongue out over lips so dry it felt as if she was licking talcum powder. 'So…why would you want to marry someone who clearly doesn't want to marry you?'

His dark-as-night gaze gleamed, making the floor of Alice's belly shudder.

'You know why.'

Alice arched one of her brows, trying to ignore the pulsing heat his words evoked deep in her feminine core. 'Revenge, Cristiano? I thought you were a civilised man.'

Melanie Milburne read her first Mills & Boon at the age of seventeen, in between studying for her final exams. After completing a Master's Degree in Education she decided to write a novel, and thus her career as a romance author was born. Melanie is an ambassador for the Australian Childhood Foundation and a keen dog lover and trainer. She enjoys long walks in the Tasmanian bush. In 2015 Melanie won the HOLT Medallion—a prestigious award honouring outstanding literary talent.

Visit the Author Profile page at millsandboon.co.uk for more titles.

THE TEMPORARY MRS MARCHETTI

BY
MELANIE MILBURNE

First Published in Great Britain 2017
By Mills & Boon, an imprint of HarperCollins*Publishers*
1 London Bridge Street, London, SE1 9GF

© 2017 Melanie Milburne

ISBN: 978-0-263-92406-0

Our policy is to use papers that are natural, renewable and recyclable
products and made from wood grown in sustainable forests. The logging
and manufacturing processes conform to the legal environmental
regulations of the country of origin.

Printed and bound in Spain
by CPI, Barcelona

THE TEMPORARY
MRS MARCHETTI

To Sarah Lewer.

Thanks for the inspiration for this novel and thanks also for being such a wonderful beauty therapist and gorgeous person.

XXXX

CHAPTER ONE

THE FIRST THING Alice noticed when she came to work that morning was the letter on her desk. Something about the officious-looking envelope with its gold embossed insignia made her skin shrink against her skeleton. Letters from lawyers always made her feel a little uneasy. But then she looked closer at the name of the firm. Why would a firm of Italian lawyers be contacting her?

She picked the letter up and her breath came to a juddering halt when she saw it was postmarked Milan.

Cristiano Marchetti lived in Milan.

Alice's fingers shook as if she had some sort of movement disorder. Surely he hadn't...*died*? A sharp pain sliced through her, her breath coming in short, erratic bursts, making not just her fingers tremble but her whole body.

Oh, no. Oh, no. Oh, no.

How had she missed that in the press? Surely there would have been an announcement for someone with Cristiano's public profile? They reported every other thing he did. The glamorous women he dated. The fading hotels he bought and rebuilt into stunning boutique accommodation all over the Mediterranean. The charity events he attended. The parties. The nightclubs. Cristiano couldn't change his shirt or shoes or socks without someone reporting it in the press.

Alice peeled open the envelope, her eyes scanning the brief cover letter, but she couldn't make any sense of it...or maybe that was because her brain was scrambled with a host of unbidden memories. Memories she had locked away for the last seven years. Memories she refused to acknowledge—even in a weak moment—because that was the pathway to regret and that was one journey she was determined never to travel. Her legs were so unsteady she reached blindly for her chair and sat down, holding the document in front of her blurry gaze.

But wait...

It wasn't Cristiano who had died. It was his grandmother, Volante Marchetti, the woman who, along with his late grandfather Enzo, had raised him since he was orphaned at the age of eleven when his parents and older brother had been killed in an accident.

Alice frowned and cast her gaze over the thick document that had come with the cover letter that named her as a beneficiary of the old woman's will. But why had his grandmother mentioned *her* in her will? Why on earth would the old lady do that? Alice had only met Cristiano's grandmother a handful of times. Volante Marchetti had been a feisty old bird with black raisins for eyes and a sharp intellect and an even sharper sense of humour. She had instantly warmed to the old lady, thinking at the time of how lucky Cristiano was to have a grandmother so spritely and fun, and had often thought of her since.

Maybe his grandmother had left her a trinket or

two—a keepsake to mark their brief friendship. A piece of jewellery or one of the small watercolour paintings Alice remembered admiring at the old lady's villa in Stresa. She began to read through the legalese with her heart doing funny little skips. So many words… Why did lawyers have to sound as if they'd swallowed a dictionary?

'Someone here to see you, Alice,' Meghan, her junior beauty therapist, said from the door.

Alice glanced at the time on her computer screen next to her appointment diary and frowned. 'But my first client isn't until ten. Clara Overton cancelled her facial. One of her kids is sick.'

Meghan waggled her eyebrows meaningfully and, lowering her voice to a stage whisper, said, 'It's a man.'

Alice had several male clients who came to her for waxing and other treatments but something told her the man waiting to see her wasn't one of them. She could feel it in her body. In her bones. In her blood. In her heartbeat. The awareness of imminent danger making a prickling sensation pass all over her flesh, as if her nerves were radar picking up a faint but unmistakable signal. A signal she had forced herself to forget. To wipe from her memory in case it caused her to regret the decision she had made back then. She pushed back her chair and stood but then decided it was better to remain seated. She didn't trust her legs. Not if she was going to come face to face with Cristiano Marchetti after all this time. 'Tell him I'll be ten minutes.'

'You can tell me yourself.'

Alice looked up to see Cristiano framed in the door, his chocolate-brown eyes as hard as two black bolts. All she could think of was how different it was seeing him in the flesh instead of a photograph in a gossip magazine or newspaper. Shockingly different. Heart-stoppingly different. *I'm-not-sure-I-can-handle-this* different.

For a moment she couldn't locate her voice. With him standing there, with his towering frame and command-ing air, her office seemed to shrink to the size of a tis-sue box. Shoulders so broad he looked as if he'd been bench-pressing bulldozers—two at a time. An abdo-men so hard and toned you could tap dance on it wear-ing stilettos and not leave a dent. Jet-black hair, thick and currently brushed back from his forehead in loose finger-groomed waves.

'Hello, Cristiano, what brings you to Alice's Won-derland of Beauty? An eyebrow-shape? Back and leg wax? Personality makeover?'

Alice knew it was crazy of her to goad him but she did it anyway. It was her defence mechanism. Sarcasm instead of emotion. Better to be cutting and mocking than to show how much his brooding presence disturbed her. It more than disturbed her. It unbalanced her. Her neatly controlled world felt as if it had been picked up and rattled like a maraca held by a maniac. The walls of her office were closing in on her. The floor was shift-ing beneath her feet like a sailboat pitching in a wild squall. The air was pulsing with crackling electricity that made her aware of every inch of her skin and every hit-and-miss beat of her heart.

His bottomless eyes roved her face as if he was look-ing for something he had lost and never thought to find again. His brow was etched in a deep frown that gave him a much more intimidating air than the way he had looked at her in the past. Back then he had looked at her with tenderness, with gentleness. With love.

A love she had thrown back in his face.

'Did you put her up to it?' he asked with a searing look that made the backs of her knees fizz as if sand were being trickled through her veins.

Alice placed her hands on the tops of her thighs below her desk so he wouldn't see their traitorous shaking. 'I presume you're referring to your grandmother?'

Something flashed in his gaze. Bitterness. Anger. Something else she wasn't ready to acknowledge, but she felt it all the same. It breathed scorching hot fire all over her body, stirring up memories. Erotic memories that made the blood in her veins pick up speed. 'Have you been in contact with her over the last seven years?' he asked in that same terse *don't-mess-with-me* tone.

'No. Why would I?' Alice gave him a pointed look. 'I rejected your proposal, remember?'

His jaw tensed so hard she could see the white tips of his clenched muscles showing through his olive tan. 'Then why has she mentioned you in her will?'

So he hadn't known about the terms of his grand-mother's will until recently? Had the old lady not told him of her plans? *Interesting.* 'No idea,' Alice said. 'I only met her a couple of times when we were…back then. I've had zero contact since.'

He glanced at the will lying in front of her on her desk. 'Have you read it?'

Alice gave him another speaking look. 'I was getting to that when you rudely barged into my office.'

His eyes nailed hers. Hard eyes. Eyes that could melt a month's supply of salon wax with a single glare. 'Let me summarise it for you. You stand to inherit a half share of my grandmother's villa in Stresa in Italy if you agree to be my wife and live with me for a minimum of six months. You will also receive a lump sum on the announcement of our engagement, which is to last no longer than one month.'

Shock hit Alice like a blow to the chest. *His...wife?*

She fumbled for the document, the sound of the pages rustling overly loud in the silence.

Engaged to him for a month? Married for six?

She cast her gaze over the words again, her breath coming in such short spark bursts it felt as if she were having an asthma attack. Her heart was beating so heavily it felt as if someone were punching it from behind. She hadn't seen any mention of marriage in her quick appraisal earlier. She'd barely had time to read any of it before he had gatecrashed into her day. Why hadn't she put on her make-up before work? Why hadn't she worn her brand-new uniform instead of this one with the eyebrow-tint stain on the right breast? Why hadn't she done her own eyebrows, for God's sake?

But there it was in black and white.

Alice was to co-inherit Volante Marchetti's summer retreat on the shores of Lake Maggiore if, and only if, she married and stayed married to Cristiano for six months. *Six months?* Six seconds would be too long. And there was the other clause. They must be engaged for no more than a month before the wedding. What sort of weird time frame was that? It shamed her that Cristiano saw the pages of the document shaking before she put it back down on the desk. But at least he couldn't see the tumult going on inside her stomach.

His wife?
Live with him?

She had been to his grandmother's villa one memorable weekend with Cristiano. Memorable because it was the first time he'd told her he loved her. Apart from her mother, no one had ever said that to her before. She hadn't said the words back because she hadn't trusted her feelings. But then, she had always been a step behind him in their relationship. She'd thought they were having a fling while she was on a brief working holiday in Europe. He'd decided it was a relationship. She'd thought it was temporary because she'd planned to go back to England and set up her own beauty spa, but he had wanted it to be permanent.

Permanent as in marriage and kids.

For as long as she could remember Alice had been against marriage—or at least for herself. After witnessing her mother go through three of them with exactly the same result: misery, subjugation, humiliation and financial ruin. She had told Cristiano a little about her background, not much, but more than she had told anyone, which made her all the more annoyed he had still gone ahead and asked her to marry him. In a crowded public place to boot, which had added a whole other layer of pressure she resented him for.

His arrogance made her furiously angry. Had he really thought she would fall upon him with a grateful squeal of *Yes!* just because he was super-rich and said he loved her and wanted to spend the rest of his life with her? How long would that love have lasted? They'd had a passionate if a little volatile relationship. How could she be sure his desire/love for her wouldn't burn out as fast as it had been ignited?

If he had truly loved her he would have accepted her no as final and settled for a less formal arrangement. People lived together for years and years without needing the formality of marriage. Why be so damn nineteen-fifties about it? A marriage certificate didn't make a relationship any more secure. In fact, it could do the very opposite, forcing women into a subservient role once kids came along from which they could never escape.

But Cristiano at heart was a traditionalist. For all of his modern male sophistication, deep down he wanted a wife and family to come home to while he built his empire. So he had given her an ultimatum. Tried to control her. Tried to manipulate her into doing what he wanted.

Marriage or nothing.

Alice had called his bluff and ended their relationship then and there, and flown back to England, never expecting to hear from him again. Well, maybe that wasn't quite true. She *had* expected to hear from him with a big apology and 'let's try again' but it hadn't happened. Showed how much he'd 'loved' her. Not enough to fight for her. Not enough to compromise.

Not that she had offered to compromise, but still.

Alice brought her gaze back up to his glittering one. 'You're surely not going to go through with this…are you?'

A smile that wasn't quite a smile courted with the edges of his mouth. 'But of course. It is what Nonna wanted. Who am I to disregard her last wishes?'

Alice frowned so hard she could have frightened off fifty units of Botox. 'What happens if I don't agree?'

'To me?' He gave a careless shrug. 'Nothing other than a few shares in the company which will pass to a relative if I don't comply with the terms of the will.'

Alice wondered how important those shares were

to him. Was his easy-come, easy-go shrug disguising deeper, far more urgent motivations? Enough to marry someone he now hated? What about the villa? It was his grandmother's home, the place where he had spent much of his childhood being raised by his grandparents. Wouldn't he want to contest such an outrageous will? Surely he wouldn't want to share it with anyone, much less her? Why would he agree to such unusual conditions? She sent her tongue out over lips so dry it felt as if she were licking talcum powder. 'So…why would you want to marry someone who clearly doesn't want to marry you?'

His dark as night gaze gleamed, making the floor of Alice's belly shudder. 'You know why.'

Alice arched one of her brows, trying to ignore the pulsing heat his words evoked deep in her feminine core. 'Revenge, Cristiano? I thought you were a civilised man.'

'I am prepared to be reasonable.'

Alice affected a laugh. That was not a word she readily associated with him. He saw the world in black and white. He didn't know the meaning of the word compromise. What he wanted he got and woe betide anyone who got in his way. Not that she could talk. Compromise wasn't her favourite word in the dictionary, either. 'Reasonable in what way?'

He held her look with one she couldn't read. 'The marriage won't be consummated.'

Not…? Alice hoped she wasn't showing any sign of the numb shock she was feeling. Not just shock. Hurt. Humiliation. Their affair had been so wildly passionate. She had never had a lover before or since who made her feel the things he had made her feel. She had all but given up dating because of it. His touch was indelibly branded on her body. No one else's touch made her flesh sing—the opposite, in fact. Her flesh crawled when someone else touched her. The last time she slept with a date, well over a year ago, she came home and showered for an hour.

'You speak as if this…this preposterous marriage is a fait accompli,' she said. 'I said it seven years ago and I'll say it again now. I am not going to marry you.'

'Six months is not a long time. At the end of it you get joint ownership of a luxury villa to do with as you please. You can sell your half or keep it. The choice is yours.'

The choice wasn't hers. How could it be? She was being forced into a marriage with a man who no longer loved her—if he ever had. What he had wanted to do back then was control her. It was what he wanted to do now. What better way to punish her for having the gall to say no to him than to chain her to him in a loveless union?

Alice wouldn't do it. *No. No. No.*

She wouldn't subject herself to the humiliation of being his trophy wife while he continued to sleep with whomever he liked. He knew…*he knew* how much she'd hated seeing her mother cheated on by each of her husbands. It had been one of the things that had impressed her about him. He believed in monogamy—or so he'd said.

But what about your business plan?

Alice had somehow become the go-to girl for wedding make-up. The girl who had sworn against marriage was preparing brides all over London for theirs. *Go figure.* Her appointment diary was booked out for months ahead for the wedding season. It was becoming the biggest source of her income, especially high-profile weddings. She had plans to buy another salon—a larger place so she could extend her business because her Chelsea salon was getting too small to handle the burgeoning wedding market.

It had been a dream of hers for months. Years, actually. The only thing holding her back was the thought of taking on a load of property debt. Debt was something that terrified her. The mere thought of it kept her awake at night. She remembered too well how it had felt as a child to have not enough money for food, for clothes, for electricity when her mother had been between relationships.

She knew she could always rent another property like this one in Chelsea, but that left her at the mercy of landlords, something she had seen too many times during her childhood. Rents could be put up and buildings suddenly sold. The business she had worked so hard to establish would be jeopardised if she didn't own the property herself.

You could sell the villa after six months and be debt-free for the rest of your life.

Alice allowed the thought a little traction. The business she had sacrificed so much for was her baby, her mission, her purpose in life. Seeing it grow and develop over the last few years had been enormously satisfying. She had built it up from just a handful of clients to now one of the busiest salons in the area. She had celebrities and minor royalty on her books. People came to her because of the standards of excellence she maintained. To achieve her dream of setting up a luxury wedding spa would finally prove she had made it.

Failing wasn't an option.

Not after using her career as the excuse for not wanting to marry Cristiano. The career she put before everything else. Relationships. Holidays. Fun. Even friendships. All of it had been sacrificed for work.

But she couldn't marry Cristiano to solve that problem for it would throw her in the middle of an even bigger one.

Alice rose from her chair with her spine steeled with resolve. 'I've made my choice. Now, if you've finished catching up on old times, I have a business to run.'

His eyes continued to tether hers as if he were waiting for her cool composure to crack. 'Are you involved with someone? Is that why you're saying no?'

Was he *still* so arrogant? *Yes.* Arrogance was hard-wired into his DNA. A man in his privileged position had no concept of why a woman wouldn't want to thrust her hand out for him to put a ring on it. He had it all: the money, the looks, the luxury lifestyle, the fast cars and exotic holiday destinations. Alice wished she had a lover to fling in his face. She considered inventing one but knew it wouldn't take him long to call her out on her lie. He wouldn't have to hunt around too far to find her social life was practically non-existent. Her work was her social life.

'I know you find it hard to believe you're irresistible because of your wealth and other…erm…assets, but I am not going to prostitute myself for the sake of an inheritance I neither asked for nor need.'

His expression gave nothing away. 'I meant what I said, Alice. It will be a marriage in name only.'

No one said her name quite the way he did. His Italian accent gave it a completely different emphasis. *Aleece*. The sound of it was like an erotic caress. It made the base of her spine shiver as if he had touched her with a brush of his warm male hand. Thinking of his hands made her want to look at them.

Don't. Don't. Don't.

But in spite of her rational brain's pleas, she looked. Those broad-spanned hands had travelled over every inch of her flesh. Those long tanned fingers had coaxed her into her first proper orgasm. They had discovered all of her erogenous zones, tortured them with such intense pleasure it had shaken her to the core of her being. She could feel the echo of it even now, as if just being in the same room as him, breathing the same air as him, made her body recognise him as her only pleasure giver.

Alice dragged her gaze upwards and collided with his. He knew. Damn it, he knew how much sensual power he had over her. She could see it in the knowing glint in his pitch-black eyes. She felt it when he sent his gaze over her body as if he too were remembering what it had felt like to hold her in his arms as she splintered into a thousand pieces of shivering, quivering ecstasy.

He lifted a hand to his jacket pocket and took out a business card and placed it on the desk next to the copy of his grandmother's will. 'My contact details should you change your mind. I'll be in London for the next week while I sort out some business affairs.'

Alice wilfully ignored the card. 'I'm not going to change my mind, Cristiano.'

I'm not. I'm not. I'm not.

A cynical smile lifted one side of his mouth. 'We'll see.'

We'll see?

What did he mean, 'We'll see'? Alice didn't get the

chance to ask him for he turned and left her office, leaving her with the lingering fragrance of his aftershave, the lemon and lime with a base note of leather that made her nostrils tingle...not to mention the rest of her body.

Meghan was bug-eyed when she came back. 'Oh, my God! You didn't tell me you knew Cristiano Marchetti. I didn't recognise him at first. He's much more gorgeous in the flesh than he is in photographs in the press. I nearly fainted when he walked past me just then and smiled at me. What did he want? Is he going to come here for treatments? Please let me do him. Can I do him? Please, please, please?'

Alice wasn't going to explain her past relationship with her employee even if Meghan was turning out to be one of the best she'd ever had. And as for Meghan 'doing him', if anyone was going to 'do him' it was going to be her. She would like nothing better than to get a pot of hot wax and strip that supercilious smile off his too-handsome face. 'He's not a client. I met him a few years ago. He just dropped in to say hi.'

'Met him as in met him and dated him?'

Alice didn't respond other than to purse her mouth. Meghan blushed and bit her lower lip. 'Sorry. I shouldn't have asked that. I know you insist on absolute confidentiality with celebrity clients. It's just he's so handsome and you never seem to date anyone and I wondered if it was because—'

'Can you get my treatment room ready for my next client?' Alice said. 'I have some urgent paperwork to see to.'

Alice blew out a breath once Meghan scuttled away. For seven years she had told herself she'd made the right decision. She had chosen her career over commitment.

Freedom over having a family. She had stood firm on her decision, not once wavering on it. Now, within her grasp was a way to finally achieve the success and financial security she had thus far only dreamt about.

Six months of marriage.

In name only.

She glanced at his business card. It seemed to taunt her with its presence.

Do it. Do it. Do it.

Alice snatched it up and tore it into as many pieces as she could and tossed them in the bin. It was kind of weird how they floated down just like a handful of confetti.

She hoped to God it wasn't an omen.

Cristiano would have had a stiff drink if he'd been a drinking man, but the death of his parents and his older brother to a drunk driver when he was eleven made him wary of using alcohol other than in strict moderation. Seeing Alice Piper again was like having his guts slashed wide open. And stomped on. The mere sight of her reopened the wound of his bitterness until he wondered how he had stood there without showing it.

He'd felt it, though. God in heaven, how he'd felt it. The blood rush. The pulse race. The adrenalin surge. The kick and punch of lust.

He had stood there and drunk in her features like a dehydrated man standing in front of a long cool glass of water. Her indifferent poise, her cornflower-blue gaze that could freeze mercury, the way she looked down her aristocratic nose at him as if he had crept in from a primeval swamp with his knuckles dragging. Her body was as lissom and gorgeous as ever—perhaps even more so. Her unusual silver-blonde hair with her naturally dark eyebrows and the creamy, ageless perfection of her skin gave her a striking appearance that never failed to snatch his breath.

Her rejection of him stung and burned and churned even after all this time. He had thought what they'd had was for ever. A once in a lifetime love. Their passionate affair had been unlike anything he'd experienced before. He'd wanted to build a future with her. A family. He'd believed it to be like the love his parents had had for each other. Like the love his grandparents had before his grandfather died. The death of his grandfather a couple of months before he met Alice had made him acutely aware of how important family was. It had been all he had thought about—having a family to replace the one he had lost so young. He'd felt ready. More than ready. He'd been twenty-seven and well established in the hotel business he had inherited from his parents. He was ready for the next phase of his life.

But Alice hadn't loved him. She had never said the words but he'd fooled himself into thinking she'd been showing it instead. How gullible he had been. How stupid to be so naively romantic when all she'd wanted was a quick fling with a foreigner to boast about with her friends.

What had his *nonna* been thinking? She had only met Alice a couple of times. Why bequeath her a share in a property worth millions and with such odd conditions attached? Six months of marriage? What sort of nonsense was this?

He hoped to God it wasn't some sneaky match-making ploy from the grave. His grandmother knew he had changed his mind about settling down. He had laughed off the suggestion every time she asked him when he was going to provide her with a great-grandchild. Nonna had expressed her disapproval of his playboy lifestyle on numerous occasions but he had always dismissed her concerns because no one was going to tell him how to run his life.

No one.

His grandmother had been disappointed when his relationship with Alice broke down. Terribly disappointed. But he had refused to talk about it. He'd had enough trouble managing his own disappointment without having to handle his grandmother's. Over the years she had stopped mentioning Alice's name knowing it would get zero response from him. Why then had she done this? Forced him back into Alice's life when it was the last thing he wanted?

The way the will was written meant if he didn't convince Alice to marry him then he would lose valuable shares in the family company to a cousin he had no time for. He wasn't going to hand over those shares only to have his cousin Rocco sell them to another party when he ran a little low on cash after playing the tables in a casino. Cristiano would rather marry his worst enemy before seeing that day dawn. He blamed himself for not telling his grandmother of Rocco's disturbing spending habits of late. But he hadn't wanted to burden her in the last months of her terminal illness.

Now it was too late.

The will had been written and now he had to convince Alice Piper to marry him.

Not that Alice was an enemy in the true sense of the word. She was a mistake he had made. A failure he wasn't particularly fond of being reminded about. He had wiped her from his memory. Every time a thought of her would enter his mind he would ruthlessly erase it like someone cleaning a whiteboard. He had lived his life since as if she had never been a part of it. As if he had never had such amazing sex with her it had made his body tingle for hours afterwards. As if he had never kissed that sensually supple mouth. As if he had never felt that mouth around him while she blew the top of his head off.

Cristiano wasn't going to let Alice think he was anything but delighted with the way his grandmother had orchestrated things. It suited him to let Alice think he was eager to put that ring on her finger and tie her to him for six months. Besides, maybe avoidance wasn't the way to handle the lingering sting of her rejection. Maybe some immersion therapy would finally end his torment.

Alice might have given him that haughty look and said no as if it were her last word on it, but this time he wasn't taking no for an answer.

CHAPTER TWO

ALICE NEITHER HEARD nor saw anything of Cristiano for the next couple of days. She had been expecting him to show up at work again, knowing him to be implacably determined when he set his mind to something. She had received a call from the lawyer handling the execution of the will, who explained some of the finer points. There was a time limit on accepting the terms. If she didn't marry Cristiano by the end of a month-long engagement the villa would be sold outside the Marchetti family. Alice wondered what Cristiano would think about that—his childhood home sold to strangers. Was that why he was pushing for this marriage? Or was it purely revenge?

On the third day without sight or sound of Cristiano, Alice got a call from her salon building's landlord, Ray Gormley. 'I know this will come as a bit of a surprise, Alice, but I've sold the building,' he said. 'The new owner is taking possession immediately. You have a few months left on your current three-year lease so it shouldn't disrupt—'

'Sold?' Alice gasped. 'I didn't even realise you had it on the market.'

'I didn't, but I got an offer I'd be a fool to refuse,'

he said. 'I'm consolidating some of my interests. This guy's bought the building next door as well. Says he's going to make them both into a luxury hotel.'

Suspicion made every hair on the back of Alice's neck stand up and fizz at the roots. 'A…a hotel?'

'Yes,' Ray said. 'You ever heard of Cristiano Marchetti? He has boutique hotels all over Europe.'

Alice's jaw was so tight she felt the tension in her neck as if someone had a noose around it—which they did. *Damn it.*

'So…let me get this straight… Marchetti approached you completely out of the blue?'

'Yes,' Ray said. 'He's been looking for suitable property in London. The UK is the only place he doesn't have a hotel. This is stage one of his British expansion.'

Alice was still trying to get her heart out of her mouth and back in her chest where it belonged. Cristiano was her new landlord? What did he plan to do? Hike up her rent so she had no choice but to marry him? She had three months left on her three-year lease. It had always worried her having such a short-term lease, which was one of the reasons she wanted to buy her own property. But Ray had always assured her he wasn't selling any time soon. His wife and three daughters were clients of hers. She had thought—stupidly thought—she was safe.

But what would happen once Cristiano took possession?

Alice ended the call and started pacing her office so hard she thought she'd go right through the floorboards to the subway below. This was absolutely outrageous. Cristiano was going to such devious lengths to bend her to his will. She wished now she hadn't torn up his card.

Not that she had forgotten his number—no matter how hard she tried to erase it, for some reason, it remained fixed in her brain. But he might well have changed it. After all, she had changed hers.

She sat back at her desk and dialled his number. She listened to it ringing and ringing, her courage just about deserting her when finally it was answered by a husky female voice. 'Hello?'

Alice's stomach dropped. 'Erm… I'm not sure if I have the right number—'

'Are you looking for Cristiano?' the young woman said.

'Erm…yes, but if he's busy I can—'

'He's right here beside me,' the woman said. 'Who will I say is calling?'

Right here beside her doing what?

Alice clenched her teeth so hard she could have bitten through a pair of tweezers. It was the middle of the day, for pity's sake. Why wasn't he at work instead of in bed with some gorgeous nymphet?

'It's Alice Piper.'

She heard the sound of the phone being handed over and couldn't stop an image forming of him lying amongst the rumpled bed linen of a hotel with a naked woman's body draped over his. 'I've been expecting you to call,' Cristiano said. 'Changed your mind yet?'

Alice gripped her phone so hard she thought her knuckles were going to burst through her skin. 'No, I have not.'

'That's a pity.' There was a note of casual amusement in his tone. 'I didn't want to have to play dirty but needs must.'

Alice's spine tightened as if someone were turning a

wrench on each and every vertebra. 'I know what you're trying to do but—'

'Come to my hotel and we'll discuss this over a drink.'

Alice wasn't going anywhere near his hotel. A hotel room was way too intimate. If she and Cristiano were alone together with a bed nearby, who knew what might happen? It wasn't him she didn't trust. It was her. Her body remembered him like a language she thought she'd long forgotten. Even now it was responding to the deep gravelly cadence of his voice, making her senses reel as if she had ingested some sort of mind-altering drug. 'I'd rather meet somewhere less…'

'Dangerous?'

The silky tone of his voice loosened the bolts on her vertebrae.

Alice pressed her lips together, trying to garner her defences. He wasn't the same man as seven years ago. He had changed. He was harder. More ruthless. More calculating and brutally tactical. She was going to have to be careful dealing with him. He wasn't in love with her now. He hated her. He wanted revenge. 'I'm not scared of you, Cristiano.'

'Perhaps not, but you're scared of how I make you feel. It's always been that way between us, has it not?'

'I felt lust for you back then. Nothing else.'

'You still feel it, don't you, *cara mia*?' His voice was a teasing feather stroking over the nerve-sensitive base of her spine.

'You're mistaken,' she said, injecting her voice with icy hauteur. 'I feel nothing for you but contempt.'

'That's a strong word for someone who once shared their body with me.'

'You know something? I didn't break your heart,' Alice said. 'I bruised your ego. That's what all this is about, isn't it? You hadn't had a woman say no to you before. You weren't in love with me. If you were you would have accepted and respected my decision not to get married.'

'That is an argument for another time,' he said with a thread of steel entering his tone. 'I want to see you to-night to discuss the rent on your salon going forward.'

Alice stiffened. It was all right for him with the millions he'd inherited when his parents were killed. She didn't have any rich relatives to hand her an empire or to give her a financial leg up when things turned ugly. Everything she had worked for had been out of her own blood, sweat and tears—and occasional tantrum. If he turned the financial screws on her now, everything she'd worked for could be compromised. Or— God forbid—even lost. 'Sometimes I wonder how you speak so fluently with all those silver spoons hanging out of your mouth.'

A pulsing silence passed.

Alice wondered if this was going to turn into one of their massive arguments. With hindsight she could see a large part of their relationship had been a power struggle. They had constantly bickered over things without anything being resolved other than in bed. Neither of them had wanted to compromise or back down from a stance. Making love had diffused the battle temporarily, but it hadn't solved the underlying issue.

He had wanted control of her and she wouldn't give it.

Cristiano released a long breath. 'I would give each and every one of those silver spoons back if I could have my parents and brother back for a day, let alone for the last twenty-three years.'

Alice suddenly felt ashamed of herself. He couldn't help his background any more than she could help hers. It was a cheap shot, similar to the ones she'd tossed at him in the past. Their verbal sparring had been a sort of foreplay. The battle of two strong wills, combined with a fierce lust for each other, had created some combustible arguments on occasion. Too many occasions. When had they ever sat down and had a discussion without one or both of them flying off in a temper? Had either of them actually listened to what the other said? Or were they too busy trying to think of a cutting comeback? 'I'm sorry. That was…unfair of me.'

'I have to go. Natalia is waiting for me.'

A dagger went to Alice's belly. She'd forgotten all about his gorgeous little bed buddy lying right beside him while he spoke to her on the phone. Jealousy rose in her like a beast that had been woken too abruptly. Giant paws of jealousy clawing at her insides, making her feel strangely hollow. Why was she feeling like this? She had no right to feel this way. She had ended their affair. She'd been the one to walk away, not him. She didn't have any rights over him now. He was a free agent to sleep with whomever he pleased. There should be no reason why the thought of him talking to her on the phone while a woman was in bed beside him should… *hurt* her so much.

'I'm sorry to force you to talk business in the middle of pleasure,' she said. 'Maybe next time turn your phone to silent so you don't get interrupted during one of your marathon sex sessions.'

There was another little silence.

Alice wished she hadn't spoken with such crisp venom. Every word she had spoken sounded as if it were painted bright green. What was wrong with her? It was crazy to give him ammunition he could use against her. If he thought for a picosecond she was jealous he would exploit it every opportunity he could.

'I'll pick you up for dinner at seven,' Cristiano said as if she hadn't spoken. 'What's your address?'

'I'm not having dinner with—'

'You will have dinner with me or I'll cancel your lease as of now.'

Alice's heart banged against her breastbone. 'You can't do that!'

'Can't I?'

She swallowed a rush of panic. She had to get control of her tongue. It wouldn't help her cause to challenge him all the time. It would only make him all the harder to manage. She could handle dinner. Sure she could. It would be a test for her. It would be proof she could spend an hour or two in his company without wanting to tear his clothes off his hot body.

Yikes. Do not even think about that body.

It was probably still naked and sweaty from bed-wrecking sex. 'Won't Natalia mind you taking out another woman for dinner?'

'No.'

Alice was frustrated by his one-word answer so went digging for more. 'She must have a very laid-back attitude to relationships to allow you to entertain other women while she's involved with you.'

'Natalia knows her place.'

'Are you going to marry her?'

'She's already married.'

Shock rendered Alice speechless for a moment. What had happened to Cristiano's conservative old-fashioned values? The Cristiano of the past would never have slept with a married woman. He'd had no time for men and women who betrayed their marital vows. He'd spoken at length about the commitment his parents had made and how he admired and respected them for staying true to it until their untimely deaths. Until death do us part had been something he had believed in to the letter.

What had changed him?

You changed him.

The thought was an uncomfortable weight in the pit of her stomach. Had she been the one to destroy his faith in relationships? But she hadn't been ready to settle down back then. Rejecting a proposal wasn't a crime, was it? Surely she'd had the right to decide whether she wanted to be married or not. It wasn't the Dark Ages, for God's sake. But the thought continued to niggle at her. Had she turned him into a casual-living playboy who had no time for commitment? These days he used women to suit his needs. He was in and out of relationships faster than a racing driver changed gears. Was he really no longer a man who longed for a wife and family of his own? And why should that make her feel so…so sad? 'Well then, I'd better get off the phone so you can get back to your grubby little affair, hadn't I?'

'I'll see you tonight,' he said and before she could think of a comeback, or tell him she wasn't going, he ended the call.

Alice dressed for dinner as if she were dressing for combat. Each layer of clothing was like putting on a suit of armour. The armour of sophistication she had been so sadly lacking seven years ago.

She sometimes wondered what Cristiano had seen in her back then. She had been twenty-one years old and newly qualified as a beauty therapist. It had been her first trip abroad without friends accompanying her. She had been on a shoestring budget while she backpacked around Europe but she'd only got as far as Italy when she'd met him in a crowded street in Milan when a sharp catch on her backpack had become caught on his clothing, as she'd brushed past.

They'd stood in the middle of the street, comically locked together by their clothes. He'd made a comment about it bringing a whole new meaning to 'hooking up with someone' and she'd laughed. Once he had untangled himself he'd insisted on buying her a coffee.

One coffee had turned into two coffees and then dinner. Instead of going back to the backpackers' centre she'd found herself accepting his offer of accommodation for the night or two she'd planned to spend in his home city. At no time had she felt any pressure to sleep with him. She was not unaware of his interest in her and she hadn't been all that good at hiding hers in him. But his respectful handling of her had impressed her. Not many healthy and virile young men of twenty-seven, as he was at that time, would have asked a woman back to his place and not expected something in return.

In the end it had been Alice who made the first move. She still remembered their first kiss. Sometimes when she closed her eyes she could still feel those firm lips moving with such urgency against hers, making every cell in her body vibrate. One kiss hadn't been enough.

Next minute she was tearing his clothes off him and all but throwing herself at him.

Her mind drifted… The drugging kisses. The phenomenal foreplay. The earth-rocking sex. The mind-bending orgasms. The electric tingling of her flesh for hours afterwards.

How had she gone so long without it?

Alice sighed and picked up her lipstick. She had never found anyone else who made her feel desire quite like that, as if she would literally die if she didn't have him. Which meant she would have to be super careful around him now. She didn't want to betray herself, to give him any hint she hadn't managed to move on with her life. Of course she had moved on with her life. She was a successful businesswoman with money in the bank…most of it borrowed, but still.

What else did she need?

The doorbell sounded and she put her lipstick in her purse and picked up her evening wrap and went to the door. Even though she was in four-inch heels Cristiano towered over her. 'You're late,' she said. 'I thought you said seven. It's half-past.'

He gave a shrug of one broad shoulder as if punctuality and common politeness were no longer of any interest to him. 'I knew you'd wait for me.'

The way he said it made it sound as if she had spent the last seven years doing exactly that. She raised her chin and sent him a look that would have soured long-life milk. 'How did you find out where I lived?'

'Your very helpful *previous* landlord.'

The slight emphasis on the word 'previous' made Alice's nerves jangle.

She wound her wrap around her shoulders, wishing she could wind it around Cristiano's neck instead. 'Where are we going to dinner?'

'Aren't you going to show me around your house first?'

Alice pinched her lips together. 'My home is hardly on a league with yours.'

He glanced around her foyer with an appraising eye. 'Nice. How long have you lived here?'

'Two years.'

'Alone?'

Alice forced herself to hold that piercing gaze even though it made every atom in her body protest. 'At the moment.'

He gave a slight nod as if her answer satisfied him on some level. 'Big place for a single girl. How many bedrooms?'

'Four.'

His ink-black brows lifted in an arc. 'Are you renting?'

Alice threw him a black look. 'Why? Are you thinking of buying it too, and jacking up the rent? Sorry to spoil your fun but I own it.' *Or at least the bank does.*

His mouth curved at one corner in a half-smile that should not have caused her heart to stumble. 'You could pay this mortgage off and have money to spare if you agree to the terms of my grandmother's will. You could expand your business as well.'

Alice's brows snapped together in a frown. How did he know she wanted to expand her business? Who on earth had he been talking to? He had an unnerving ability to gain information about her. And read her mind. Not to mention her body.

Oh, dear God, why wasn't her body ignoring him? Damn it.

Her body was a traitor. It remembered him too well. It only had to be within touching distance and it went haywire. It was as if the last seven years hadn't happened. All her nerves were screaming out for his touch like starstruck teenage fans at a boy-band concert. 'My business plans are absolutely no concern of yours. Nor indeed are my private ones.'

His eyes moved over her body in an assessing sweep that made her insides coil with lust. She knew that look. The look that said, *I want you and I know you want me. And I can prove it.*

'It must get a bit lonely at times, living in this big old house by yourself, *si*?'

'I'm not one bit lonely.'

He released a small puff of air that had cynicism riding on its backdraft. 'Sure you're not.' He was suddenly standing closer than she'd realised. Had she been so mesmerised by his gaze she hadn't detected him closing the distance between them? He reached out and picked up a tendril of her hair and wound it around the length of his index finger. It was too late to step back.

Why the hell hadn't she stepped back?

Every nerve root on her scalp was tingling from the tether of his touch.

'Have you missed me, *cara*?' His voice was a deep, seductive burr of sound that sucker-punched her self-control.

Alice had to swallow three times to locate her voice. *Three times!* As it was she only just stopped herself from giving a betraying whimper. 'If you don't let go of me this instant I'll file my nails on your cheek. Got it?'

His mouth curved in an indolent smile and he wound

her hair a little tighter. 'I'd much rather you'd rake them down my back.'

His incendiary words sent a shockwave of lust through her body. She swore she could feel the echo of where he had been in the past—the thickened length of him driving into her until they both lost control. Her blood simmered in her veins, rushing through her system as if it were on fire.

Get control. Get control. Get control.

The words were sounding an alarm in her brain but her body was blatantly ignoring it. Her body swayed towards his…or maybe his moved closer. His muscle-packed thighs brushed hers, reminding her of all the times they had trapped hers beneath their sensual power and superior strength. Sex with Cristiano had always had an element of danger to it. The dark unknowable power of it. The uncontrollable force of it had thrilled and frightened her in equal measure. Her body felt things with him it had never felt before or since. Not even close. She was spoilt now for anyone else.

Another good reason to hate him.

Alice pushed back against his chest even though it tugged cruelly on her hair. 'In your dreams, buddy.'

Cristiano's gaze had a mocking glint to it. 'I could have you in a heartbeat and you damn well know it.'

'Ah, but you don't want me, remember?' Alice said with an arch look. 'A marriage in name only, wasn't it?'

A whip-quick flicker of tension moved across his mouth. He stepped back and held open the door. 'We'll lose the booking if we don't make a move. I had to pull strings to secure it.'

'You're good at that, aren't you, Cristiano? Pulling strings to get people to do what you want?' Alice gave him a sugar-sweet smile on her way past him in the doorway. 'What a pity you can't get *me* to toe the line.'

He captured her forearm in the steel bracelet of his long, strong fingers, tugging her around so his gaze clashed with hers. His eyes were onyx-dark and brooding with indomitable purpose. 'I haven't finished with you yet. But once I am, I swear to God you'll be on your knees begging me to marry you.'

Alice flashed him a look of pure defiance and wrenched out of his hold, rubbing her arm as if it had been scorched. Which it had. Why, oh, why was it so damn exciting sparring with him? She hadn't felt like this in years. Alive. Switched on after a long time on pause. Running at breathtaking speed instead of idling. It was nothing short of exhilarating. 'You think you can bully me into doing what you want? Try it and see what happens.'

His eyes dipped to her mouth, setting off a feverish chain of reaction in her body. Only he could do that. Make her hot for him by looking at her. 'You'd be a fool to throw away this chance to build your asset base,' he said. 'Don't let emotion get in the way of a good business deal.'

'Who are you to lecture me about emotion?' Alice said. 'You're the one who was in love with me, not me with you, and now you're punishing me because I'm about the only person on this planet who has the backbone to stand up to you and—'

'I wasn't in love with you.'

The words stung like a hail of rubber bullets. Alice blinked. Swallowed. Blinked again. *Not in love with her?* Not even a little bit? Why that should bother her she didn't want to examine too closely. 'Right, well then, that's good to know. At least I did you a favour then in rejecting your proposal. We would've been divorced by now otherwise and think how much that would've cost you.'

He opened the passenger door for her, jerking his head towards the vacant seat like a police officer taking in a suspect for interrogation. 'Get in.'

Alice straightened her shoulders, throwing him a glare that could have stripped ten years of graffiti off a council estate wall. 'Ask nicely.'

A muscle flicked in his jaw and his eyes smouldered like black coals. 'You know what will happen if you push me too far.' His tone was silk wrapped around a will of steel.

Alice did know and it was perverse of her to keep doing it. But she couldn't seem to help herself. It was an urge she couldn't control. She wanted to push him. She wanted to bait him. To break him. To reduce him to his most primal. A spurt of excitement lit like a wick inside her, sending a radiant heat coursing through her body. Her breasts tingled as if they were preparing themselves for the possessive cup of his hands. Her thighs trembled with the memory of his intimate invasion, her blood stirring into a frenzied whirlpool that made her aware of every feminine muscle contracting and releasing in her groin.

Oh, how she had missed this!

No one made her feel so…so energised. So vital. So…*aroused.*

She kept her gaze locked on his. The air was so charged with static she could hear it like a fizzing roar in her ears. 'What are you going to do, Cristiano? Lug

me over your shoulder and carry me off like the cave-
man you really are underneath that smart Armani suit?'

Another ripple of tension passed over his rigidly set
mouth, his eyes blazing as they tussled with hers. His
hand left the top of his car door and snared one of hers
before she could do anything to counter it—if she had
wanted to, that was—ruthlessly tugging her towards
him so there was barely a breath of air between their
bodies. Alice could feel the slight protrusion of his belt
buckle digging her in the stomach, a shockingly erotic
reminder of the latent male power stirring just below it.

'Been a long time between drinks, has it, *cara*?' he
asked in that dangerously smooth tone.

Alice huffed out a laugh but it didn't come out quite
as convincing as she would have liked. It sounded
breathless. Uncertain. Out of its depth. 'You don't get
to hear about my love-life. It's none of your business.'

His fingers subtly tightened around her wrist, his
touch a band of fire that sent lightning-fast currents of
hot electricity straight to her core. 'It will become my
business once we're married next month.'

Next month? Eek!

Alice elevated her chin, sending him a look of un-
diluted disdain. 'You seem to have a big problem understanding the concept of the word no. I'm. Not.
Marrying. You.'

His top lip lifted in a sardonic curl. 'You want me
so bad I can smell it.'

Alice disguised a quick swallow. She could smell
it too. The musk and salt of arousal coming off both
of them like a black magic potion. A swirling wicked
spell. Its dangerous tentacles were wrapping around

her body, coiling like a serpent, strangling her resolve until it was gasping for air.

Only he could do this to her. Make her so wild with need she forgot everything but the greedy hunger in her body clamouring for satiation.

His thighs were flush against hers, the swell of his erection so powerfully male—so blatantly, unashamedly male—it made every feminine cell in her body roll over and beg. Somehow—miraculously—she managed to conjure up a mocking smile. 'That ego of yours is so big it deserves its own postcode. Or its own government.'

A spark of amusement lit his gaze and his fingers around her wrist loosened slightly, his thumb stroking in a fainéant movement over the hummingbird leap of her pulse. 'Did you miss what we had together?'

Alice schooled her features into a mask of cool indifference. 'Not a bit.'

His probing gaze kept hers captive. 'So why haven't you had a serious relationship since?'

How on God's sweet earth did he know that?

Alice arched a brow. 'None that *you* know about. Unlike you, I don't live my life followed by paparazzi documenting every time I sneeze.'

'When was your last relationship?'

She flicked her eyelids upwards. 'Oh, for God's sake, what is this? Twenty questions?'

His gaze didn't waver. 'A long time, then.'

Alice pursed her lips and then released them with a rush of air. 'Are we having dinner or are we going to stand here and swap dating histories? I can get you a list of name and numbers if you'd like? I could even do a printout of some of their messages and emails if that gives you a hard-on.'

Cristiano put his hand back on top of the rim of the car door. 'That won't be necessary.'

Alice brushed past him to get in the car, shooting him a glare through the windscreen when he strode in front of the car to take his place behind the wheel. He started the engine with a powerful roar and entered the traffic with a quick glance over his shoulder, the G-force sending her back against the butter-soft leather seat.

Why did his driving always remind her of sex?

The thunderous growl of his engine, the thrusting of the gears, the press on the brakes and the push down on the throttle made her think of all the times he had taken her to bed—or other places—and driven them both to paradise.

Alice's gaze went to his hands holding the steering wheel with such indolent confidence, the long, tanned fingers with their dusting of dark hair doing all sorts of strange things to her insides. What was it about those hands that made her squirm with need? How was she to get through an evening with him? Sitting across the table with him at a restaurant, for God's sake?

How the hell had he got her to agree to dinner?

That was one of the scariest things about Cristiano Marchetti. He had an unnerving ability to get her to do things she had no intention of doing.

But...

That tricky little 'but' kept gnawing at the wainscoting of her mind. But what if she did agree to it? Six months was nothing. It would flash past. And at the end of it she would be set up financially. For life. She could build her wedding spa with money to spare. She could buy the best equipment, lavishly decorate the place without the limitations of a budget. She could take a holiday—something she hadn't done in years.

Alice chewed it over… He was expecting her to say no. But wait a minute… What if he didn't *want* her to say yes? What if he was only making all this fuss to make her think he was keen to get that ring on her finger?

She smiled a secret smile. She would string him along for a while longer and then she would call his bluff and expose his true motivations.

Married for six months to her mortal enemy?

Game on.

CHAPTER THREE

CRISTIANO OPENED AND closed the fingers of his right hand where they were gripping the steering wheel. He could still feel the hot tingle of Alice's skin against his fingertips. His lust for her was pounding like a jungle drum deep in his body. He ached with it. Burned with it. Vibrated with it. No one but her could reduce him to this. To stir in him such primitive, out of control longings. Longings he had never felt for anyone else. Longings that made a mockery of the sex he'd had before her and since.

Not that he hadn't had great sex over the years. He had. Many times. He'd made a point of it—using every sexual encounter to drive home the point to himself he could live without her.

It was just that in comparison to what he'd shared with Alice…well, it wasn't in the same league. Her body, her touch, her wildcat-on-heat response to him triggered something in him. Something indefinable. Something that made his flesh shudder in reaction when she came near. Something that, even now, with her sitting less than a half a metre away, he could feel moving through his body like the aftershocks of an earthquake.

He had to get her out of his system.

He had to.

He could no longer tolerate the rush of adrenalin every time he saw a silver-blonde head in the crowd and the savage drop of his gut afterwards when he realised it wasn't her. He had to prove to himself he was over her.

Was this why his *nonna* had set her will up this way? To help him move past the five-foot-six blonde road-block in his life? To force him to confront the failure he would give anything to forget?

Cristiano had made a promise to himself not to sleep with Alice. *Look, but don't touch.* But how long was that going to last? He was barely keeping his hands off her now. All he had to do was reach over and stroke his hand down the slim flank of her thigh peeping out from above the knee-high hem of her little black dress.

His fingers twitched against the steering wheel. His groin growled when she crossed one long leg over the other, her racehorse-slim ankle moving up and down as if she were feeling the same restless agitation he was feeling.

Of course she was.

Cristiano allowed himself an internal smile. His ego had nothing to do with it. He could see the struggle she was having controlling her desire for him. He had felt it from the moment he'd stepped into her office and seen her sitting like a starchy schoolmistress behind that desk. She'd used the desk as a barrier. She hadn't trusted herself to get too close to him. She knew her body would betray her as his was doing to him. It was the way they were together. Match and tinder. Spark and flame. Trigger and explosion.

It was only a matter of time before he had her where he wanted her. Begging him. Clawing at him with those little wildcat claws. Gasping his name between panting breaths as he showed her what she'd been missing. What *he'd* been missing. Dear God, how he'd missed it! Missed her. The feistiness of her. The razor-sharp wit of her tongue. The flashpoint temper and the come-and-get-me teasing that had made him feel as if he were living on the edge of a vertiginous cliff.

The way her body felt around him when he drove in to the hilt.

Getting her to marry him was his goal, not sleeping with her…although if what he had seen from her so far was any indication, sleeping with her might happen sooner rather than later. A little financial blackmail was not his usual modus operandi, but he had to get her married to him otherwise his shares would be lost.

Not to mention the villa.

He couldn't lose that. It was the place where his father had grown up. It was where Cristiano had spent numerous happy family holidays before his parents' and brother's death. It was his home for the rest of his childhood and adolescence, the place where overnight he had grown from boy to man. Losing the villa would be like losing even more of his family than he had lost already.

Why had his grandmother done such an outrageous thing as to force him to share it with Alice?

He didn't need a conscience right now. Six months would pass before he knew it. He would insist on Alice living with him because he wasn't going to let the press get wind of there being anything amiss with his 'marriage'. No way was Alice Piper going to make a laughing stock out of him in the daily tabloids. He would enjoy making her act the role of devoted wife. It would be amusing to see her push against the boundaries he laid down.

'So, we'll have a nice dinner and discuss this situation we find ourselves in,' Cristiano said after a time.

'Discuss?' Alice's voice held a generous note of scorn. 'You don't discuss. You command.'

He sent her a smiling glance. 'And as my wife you will obey.'

Even from the other side of the car he could feel the heat coming off her livid blue glare. 'They have rewritten the marriage ceremony since the nineteen-fifties, you know. Women no longer have to obey their husbands. Not that you're going to be my hus—'

'We'll have a month-long engagement as the will specifies,' Cristiano said. 'You either marry me at the end of it or find yourself paying a rent you can ill afford.'

Her face was a picture of impotent outrage, almost puce instead of her natural creamy colour. 'You...you *bastard.*' Her hands curled into tight little balls as if she was tempted to fly at his face and was only just stopping herself. 'You scheming bastard.'

He gave a careless shrug. 'Sticks and stones.'

It was a while before she said anything. Cristiano wondered if she were thinking things over, running her mind over the figures, so to speak. She ran a good business, he had to give her that, but it would not survive a big hike in rent. And to get her to do what he wanted, he was prepared to go as high as it took.

Whatever it took.

'Why engaged for a month?' she said. 'If you're in such a hurry to get a ring on my finger then why not frogmarch me to a register office right away?'

'I'm not having anyone speculate on why we're not having a proper wedding, that's why,' Cristiano said, wondering if she was speaking figuratively or if she was changing her mind about marrying him.

'But you can't really mean to go to such lengths? I mean, a wedding is a big expense.'

'I can afford it.'

There was another silence.

'All right.' Her breath came out in a whoosh. 'You win. I'll marry you.'

Cristiano hadn't expected such a rapid capitulation. He'd thought she would have fought it a little longer and a little harder. But then he wondered if she had a counter plan. She was clever. Whip-smart and streetwise. What devious plan had she cooked up? Did she intend to make him suffer every minute they were engaged? Did she really think she could outmanoeuvre him? He smiled another private smile.

Who knew this could be so much fun?

'I'm glad you're starting to see the positive side of our circumstances. It's a win-win for both of us, *si*?'

The look she gave him would have sent a swarm of wasps running for cover. 'Everyone's going to know this is a farce the moment we're seen out in public together.'

'Ah, but that's where you're wrong, *tesoro*,' Cristiano said. 'We're going to act like a happy and devoted couple at all times and in all public spaces.'

A spluttering noise came from her side of the car. 'Not on your life—'

'Apart from when we're alone,' he continued as if she hadn't spoken. 'Then the claws can come out. I'm quite looking forward to it, actually.' He gave her another goading smile. 'It will be like old times, yes?'

Her eyes were spitting chips of blue ice, her mouth set in such a tight line her lushly shaped lips all but disappeared. Her whole body seemed to be shaking with rage. He could feel the vibration of it from his side of the car.

'Why are you doing this? Why? Why? Why?'

Why was he?

Good question. It wasn't just the shares, although that was a big part of it. It was more the sense of wanting to rewrite the past. To be in control this time. To be in charge of his emotions and passions. To be the one who told her when it was over, not the other way around. He was not going to be that person ever again—the person left behind. He had been that person as a child of eleven.

Left behind by his family.

The shock of that loss had never left him. Sometimes he could still feel that claw of despair in his chest, dragging, tearing at his organs. That terrible day when his grandparents had delivered the devastating news of the death of his parents and brother, he had felt as if he were the only person left on the planet.

Alone.

Abandoned.

Isolated.

It was the same feeling he'd felt when Alice walked out on his proposal. He stood in the middle of that crowded restaurant feeling as if a wall of thick glass were separating him from everyone else. No one could reach him. He could not reach them. He was blocked. Imprisoned in a cage along with his frustrated hopes and shattered dreams.

'We have unfinished business, Alice.'

'No. We. Don't.' Her words came out like hard pellets. 'Our business is finished. Kaput. Over. Dead and buried.'

Cristiano parked the car before he swivelled in his seat to look at her. She was sitting with her arms stiffly folded, her legs crossed, and her ankle jerking up and down as if she had a tic. 'It's not though, is it, *cara*? It's not one little bit finished.'

Her eyes met his and her throat moved up and down over a swallow like a small creature moving under a rug. But then she lowered her gaze to a point just below the knot of his tie. He heard her take a breath that sounded more like a shudder than a breath. 'You always did play dirty.'

'I play to win,' he said. 'So do you. It's why we clash so much.'

Her eyes came back to his. Hard. Bright. Flashing with such palpable rage he could feel it throbbing in the air that separated them. 'I won't let you win this, Cristiano. You might be able to blackmail me into marrying you, but you can't make me fall in love with you. That's what you want, isn't it? You want me to fall in love with you and then throw it back in my face like I threw back yours.'

'On the contrary, falling in love with me would be most inadvisable,' Cristiano said. 'Falling into bed with me? Well, that may be worth considering.'

Her eyes went as wide as the steering wheel he was resting his arm across. 'But you said you don't—'

'A man can change his mind, can't he?'

Her mouth opened and shut a couple of times, two flags of pink riding high on her cheekbones. 'I'm not going to sleep with you. I don't care how much you blackmail me.'

'Fine. Probably better that way.' He opened his door and proceeded to get out. 'I can get my needs met elsewhere.'

She sprang out of the car before he could get round to her side. 'Oh, no, you don't,' she said, hands on hips. 'You don't get to cheat on me. No way. If you can have lovers then so can I.'

Cristiano slowly shook his head as if dealing with a small, wilfully disobedient child. 'No. I'm the one who makes the rules. You follow them.'

She came at him with a pointed finger, drilling him in the chest like a tiny outraged jackhammer. 'I'm not obeying any of your stupid rules. I'm going to do what I damn well like and you can't stop me.'

Cristiano captured her hand, every cell in his body aching to tug her flush against him and show her what she was doing to him. But he was biding his time, waiting for her to come to him, as he knew in his bones she would. Her fiery nature stirred the banked-down embers of his. The heat was rising in a wildfire of lust, thundering through him like a runaway train on a steep decline.

He wanted her.

Oh, how he *wanted* her.

It was a thirst he couldn't quench with anyone else. A hunger that refused to be satisfied with another's touch. She was in his blood. In his body. She was a fever that had lain dormant until he had walked into her beauty salon and seen her sitting there with that coolly indifferent look on her face.

She wasn't indifferent to him. Not one little bit. He could see it in her eyes, the way they kept darting to his mouth and the way her tongue swept over her lips as if recalling the taste and feel of his crushed to its softness.

Cristiano slid one hand up her warm, silky smooth thigh. 'If we weren't in a public place I would take you right here and now.'

She pushed back from him as if he had suddenly burst into scorching flames. 'Get away from me.'

'Careful, Alice,' he said. 'We're in public. It's time to behave yourself.'

Her eyes went to needle-thin slits, her body visibly quaking with fury. 'Just you wait until I get you alone.'

He smiled and gave a mock shiver of delight. 'I can hardly wait.'

Alice was so angry she could barely read the menu. A red mist was before her eyes at the way he had turned things around so deftly. So he *did* want to marry her. But why? What did he hope to achieve? A bunch of stupid old shares he probably didn't need? She didn't buy that for a second. He wanted to marry her to punish her. To humiliate her.

But the more she thought about the long-term benefits for the short-term pain, she realised she really didn't have a choice. If she wanted to reach the pinnacle of success she had always dreamed of then this was the way to do it, and far quicker than she could ever have imagined.

She remembered his grandmother's villa. That lakeside villa was not some modest little run-down holiday shack. That villa was a luxury resort complete with lush gardens and trickling fountains and marble statues and a swimming pool big enough to set an Olympic record. If she walked away from a gift like that she would be certifiable.

Besides, the old lady had liked her and Alice had

liked her. A lot. She didn't want any paranormal consequences if she didn't accept the bequest with good
grace. It was the sensible, respectful thing to do.

The only trouble was Cristiano was part of the deal.

*The man who could make her come on the spot by
looking at her with those sinfully sexy eyes.*

Alice shifted in her seat, painfully aware of the swollen excitement of her body. For a moment there she'd
thought he was going to kiss her. His body had been
so close to hers she'd felt his warmth, smelt his lemon
and lime and hint of leather scent that wreaked such
havoc on her senses. She had seen the way his eyes
had dipped to her mouth, lingering there as if recalling the way her lips had responded to his in the past.
The even more shocking thing was she'd wanted him
to. So much her whole body had ached to feel that firm
mouth come crashing down on hers. To take the choice
away from her.

What was wrong with her?

But wasn't that what he wanted? To show how weak
she was when it came to him? He knew her as a mae-
stro knew a difficult instrument. He knew what chords
to strike, what strings to pluck, what melodies to play.

Alice was annoyed for thinking she could outsmart
him. When had calling his bluff ever worked? He wasn't
the type of man to be manipulated. He enjoyed power
too much to allow anyone else to control him.

The truth was she had been a little shocked when
he'd let her go seven years ago. Shocked and hurt. She'd
thought he'd wanted her too much to let her go without
a fight. She'd thought he desired her so much he would
have moved heaven and earth and planets and whole
galaxies to get her back. She'd thought he would con-

tact her within a day or two when he calmed down and apologise for pressuring her with that public proposal.

But he hadn't contacted her.

Not a single word. No phone call. No text or voicemail message. No flowers. No cards. Days, a week, two weeks went past and still she heard nothing from him. But then she saw a press photo of him in a nightclub in Milan with a bevy of beautiful women draped all over him. And a day later another photo with just the one woman—his new mistress. A gorgeous international model. It had driven a stake through her chest to see him getting on with his life as if she had never been the 'only woman in the world' for him. What nonsense. He hadn't loved her at all. He had wanted to own her. To control her.

As if that was ever going to happen.

He might be able to stir her hormones into a fizzing frenzy, but no way was Alice going to let him take over her life. She would marry him to get what she wanted.

You want him.

It was an inconvenient truth but she would deal with it. She had willpower, didn't she? A month-long engagement was the first hurdle. It wasn't a long period of time. Anyway, she would be at work most of the time. September was still a busy time. And he had his little thing on the side. *Grrr.* Alice wasn't going to show she was jealous about his nubile little Natalia. If he wanted to play around then why should she care? If she was going to be Cristiano's fiancée and then wife, then she would be the worst fiancée and wife in the world.

Alice smiled a *you-ain't-seen-nothing-yet* smile and picked up her wine glass and drained it in a couple of noisy swallows. She put it down on the starched white tablecloth with a distinctive thud. 'Nice drop. So, when do I get a big rock on my finger? Or have you got your old one stashed away in your pocket?'

His dark eyes pulsed like the shimmer off a heat-wave. 'I do, actually.' He reached inside his jacket and took out the ring he'd bought her seven years ago.

Alice took it from the centre of his outstretched palm and slipped it on. 'Slipped' being the operative word. It was loose and the heavy diamond slipped around her finger so it was facing downwards. Those few pounds she'd carried at twenty-one had thankfully been whit-tled off with diet and exercise. The ring hadn't suited her hand back then and it didn't now. Which was per-fectly fine because she didn't want it to suit. It wasn't going to be there long enough for her to worry about it being clumsily big.

'Lovely. I'll be the envy of all my friends.' She looked up to see a furrowed frown between his eyes and gave him a guileless blink. 'Is something wrong?'

His frown relaxed but his mouth lost none of its tight-ness. 'There are some domestic things to discuss. Like where we'll live for the next four weeks before the wed-ding.'

Alice straightened her posture. 'I'm not living with you. I have my own house and—'

'It will seem odd for us not to cohabit. You can move in with me at my hotel or I can move in with you. Your choice.'

Her choice? What a joke. Alice raised her chin to a combative height. 'What if I say no?'

His unwavering gaze made something in her belly turn over. 'How about a compromise? A few nights at your place, a few nights at mine.'

Alice snorted. 'Compromise? You mean you actually *know* what that word means?'

He ignored her taunt. 'After we're married we'll have to live under the one roof, and since my base is in—'

'I'm not moving to Italy so you can squash that thought right now. I have work commitments. I'm solidly booked till Christmas.' Not solidly, but heavily. Not that she was going to tell him that. Why should she give up her career when he wasn't giving up his?

A muscle moved in his jaw. In. Out. In. Out. 'I want you with me. Six months, that's all the will requires. I won't accept any other arrangement.'

Alice gave a mock pout and leaned forward as if she were talking to a spoilt child. 'Oh, poor baby, did you want to have it all your own way?' She sat back with a resounding thump and folded her arms. 'Sorry. No can do.'

Cristiano's eyes hardened. 'Must you always be so damn obstinate?'

'Me, obstinate?' Alice laughed. 'You win the prize for that. A mule has nothing on you. Your heels are dug so deep in the ground you could drill for oil.'

He gave her a droll look. 'I've booked a flight to Italy this Friday. We'll stay the weekend in Stresa so you can get acquainted with your new property. Think of it as a trial honeymoon.'

Honeymoon?

Alice's stomach dropped like an anchor. 'I presume you mean for the sake of appearances?'

A ghost of a smile flirted with the edges of his mouth. 'That depends.'

She disguised a lumpy swallow. 'On what?'

'On whether you have the self-discipline to say no to me.'

Alice gave him a look that would have withered poison ivy. 'Not going to happen, Italian boy. You're getting your needs met elsewhere, remember?'

'Natalia is my personal assistant.'

Alice arched her brow. 'And what, pray tell, does she personally assist you with? Your sex life?'

A smile cocked one side of his mouth, making his eyes crinkle attractively at the corners. Too attractively. So attractively she was having trouble keeping her eyes off it and remembering how sexy it had once felt against her own. 'You're jealous.'

Alice gave a honk of a laugh. 'Yes, of course I am. I'm just so in love with you I can barely stand it. I've been waiting all these years for you to show up and take me back to chain me barefoot to the kitchen sink and make me pregnant.'

His smile disappeared to be replaced by a thin line of white. 'I would've given you a good life, Alice. Better than the one you've got now.'

Alice helped herself to more wine, not caring it was going to her head. 'I love my life. I have my own business. I have my own house. Money. Friends.'

'But you're not happy.'

She stabbed a finger in his direction. 'You know what that is you're doing right there? It's projection. What you're really saying is *you're* not happy.'

'I will be happy when this six months is over,' he said, through tight lips. 'My grandmother had no right to meddle in my affairs.'

Alice toyed with her glass, wondering why his grandmother had taken it upon herself to orchestrate things the way she had. Hadn't Volante Marchetti realised how pointless it would be locking her and Cristiano together? They hated each other. They fought like cage fighters. What good would it serve? They would only end up worse enemies than before.

She realised then, she hadn't yet expressed her condolences for his loss. She knew how much he adored his grandmother. It was another thing she had liked about him—how much he respected the elderly and saw them as gatekeepers of wisdom. 'You must miss her terribly.'

He released a long sigh that sounded rough around the edges. 'Yes.'

'Was she ill for long or was it a sudden—?'

'Pancreatic cancer,' he said. 'Four months from diagnosis to death.'

'It must have been an awful shock.'

'It was, but less so than my parents' and brother's death. She was eighty-five and frail. She was ready to go.'

Alice wondered if he was close to his extended family. He hadn't spoken much about his family back in the day. She knew there were an uncle and an aunt and a few cousins scattered about. But having lost every member of his immediate family must surely be extremely painful, even now. She wasn't that close to her mother, and, while she had some contact with her father since they reconnected a couple of years ago, her extended family were not the sort of people she associated with. But even so, Alice couldn't imagine being all alone in the world.

The waiter came to take their order, and once he left, Cristiano switched the subject as if he didn't want to linger on the subject of his grandmother's passing.

'There are some legal things to see to. I presume you won't object to a prenuptial agreement?'

'No, why should I?' Alice shot him a *don't-call-me-a-gold-digger* glare. 'I want to protect my own assets.'

'Fine. I'll have the papers drawn up and make an appointment for tomorrow.'

He was moving things along so quickly Alice wondered if he was worried she would back out at the last minute and was taking measures so she couldn't. 'How are you going to handle the press on this?' she asked. 'I mean, who is going to buy this is a genuine love match?'

His expression gave nothing away. 'We have a history which makes the lie all the more believable. Everyone loves a love-wins-out-in-the-end story.'

'Well, don't expect me to get all gussied up for the wedding,' Alice said. 'Me in one of those big meringue dresses? Not my thing at all.'

There was a moment or two of silence.

The air seemed to ring with her words as if testing their veracity. Just as well Cristiano didn't know about the stash of bridal magazines she had at home. Dozens of them. It was a silly little pastime but she rationalised it by insisting it helped her follow make-up trends for her clients. And it was a tax deduction.

'You might never get married again,' he said. 'Why not go to town on this one chance to be a princess for the day?'

'You're darn right I'm not getting married again,' Alice said. 'I'm going to be drinking champagne by the bucket once our marriage is over.'

Once our marriage is over.

It was strange to say those words when most people entered marriage thinking it was going to be for ever.

Weddings had never been Alice's fantasy. She hadn't dressed up as a bride as a child or pored over bridal magazines as a teenager. She'd always seen marriage as a trap to keep women enslaved to the patriarchy. A tool to maintain male privilege in society. Women lost financial traction once they married and had kids and few ever truly regained it. She had seen her mother lose self-esteem and money with every failed relationship. Alice had lived in near poverty too often as a child to ever think of getting married herself.

But lately, Alice had dealt with a lot of brides. Happy brides. Brides who were madly in love with their men and their men with them. The excitement of building a future with a man who loved you and wanted to spend his life with you had rubbed off on her even though she'd thought it never would. Every time she prepared a bride's make-up for her big day she wondered what it would be like to be a bride herself. To dress in a beautiful gown and have her hair and make-up done. To walk into a flower-filled church and say the vows that couples for centuries had been saying to each other.

A lot of the brides she had done still came into the salon as regular clients. It might be an isolated statistic, but so far not one of them had separated or divorced. On the contrary, they seemed happier and even more radiant. Several of them had babies and young children now.

It made Alice wonder if her bias was a little unjustified.

'What will you do with your share of the villa once we get an annulment?' he asked.

An annulment? Wait, he was actually *serious* about not sleeping with her? But why the hell not? Alice knew she wasn't going to be asked to strut down a catwalk any time soon but she hadn't had any mirrors explode when she'd walked past, either. 'Of course I'll sell my share. It's the money I want, not the property. I wouldn't be able to maintain a property that size—even a half share in it—not while working and living in London. Old places like that cost a fortune in upkeep.'

Cristiano gave a single nod as if that made perfect sense. But Alice couldn't help feeling he was disappointed in her answer. What did the villa mean to him? Would he want to buy her share back once their marriage came to an end? Her conscience began to prickle her. Why should he be made to pay for something that should rightfully be his?

'Were you expecting your grandmother to leave her villa entirely to you?' Alice asked after a moment.

'Yes and no.' His expression was masked. 'I have enough property of my own without hankering after that old place. But that doesn't mean I want to see it sold to strangers.'

'It must hold a lot of memories for you.'

'It does. Both good and bad.' He reached for his water glass but he didn't drink from it. Instead, his index finger scrawled a swirly clockwise pattern on the condensation on the side of the glass. 'It was a happy place before it became a sad place. Over time it became happy again, mostly due to my grandparents' commitment to making my childhood and adolescence as normal as they could under the circumstances.'

Alice chewed at her lip. When had she ever talked to him like this? *Really* talked? She had tried asking him about his childhood seven years ago but he had always brushed the topic aside. Told her he didn't like talking about it. She had respected that and left well alone. But now she wondered if that had been a mistake. 'It must have been devastating to lose your family like that...'

'And then some.' He let out a small breath and began drawing on his glass in an anti-clockwise fashion this time. 'I still remember the day my parents and brother were killed... I was staying overnight with my grandparents as I'd caught a stomach bug and couldn't go to the party they were attending.' His mouth came up on one side in a rueful slant and his finger left the glass. 'Lucky me. Saved by a rotavirus.'

Alice swallowed against a knot of emotion for the little boy he had been. How lonely and desperate he must have felt to have his family wiped out like that. Never to see them again. Never to have the opportunity to say the words he'd wanted to say. All the questions kids ask their parents about themselves—the funny anecdotes of infancy and childhood that only a parent can relay.

Why hadn't she asked more about how he'd felt when they'd dated? Why had she let him fob her off? Had he been riddled with survivor guilt? Wondering why he had been spared and not his brother? How could it not have an effect on him even now? He had grown up without the most important people by his side. Yes, his grandparents were marvellous substitutes, but they could only ever be his grandparents. He carried the wound of loss in every fibre of his being.

'I wish I'd asked you more about your childhood in the past... You always seemed so...so reluctant to talk about it and I didn't want to pry.'

'I hardly ever talked about it, even to my grandparents.' He continued to stare at his glass, his brow creased in a slight frown. 'I thought it was my family coming back when I heard the car. But it was a police vehicle. My grandfather broke the news to me...'

The trench of his frown deepened.

'It's weird, but I never really thought about that until a few years ago. How it would have been for him to hear his only son and daughter-in-law and eldest grandson had died and then have to break that news to me in a calm and controlled and caring manner. He was so... so unbelievably strong. For me. For Nonna. I never saw him cry but I sometimes heard him. Late at night, in his study, long after Nonna and I and the staff had gone to bed. It was a terrible sound.'

Alice reached across the table and placed her hand over his large warm tanned one where it was resting on the snowy-white tablecloth. He looked up when she touched him, his gaze shadowed by memories. By sadness. Bone-deep sadness. 'I'm so sorry...' she said.

He pulled his hand away and leaned back in his chair. 'It was a long time ago. I never lacked for anything. My grandparents made sure of that.'

Alice wondered if anyone—even grandparents as loving and stable as Cristiano's—could ever make up for the loss of one's parents and only brother. Children were known to be fairly resilient, but how hard it must have been for him to know he would never see his parents and brother again. He had all the money anyone could wish for and yet he couldn't bring back his loved ones. Was that why he was so controlling? So rigid and uncompromising? Was that why he had insisted on marrying her seven years ago and wouldn't take no for an answer? He had wanted stability because he had lost it in childhood.

But Alice hadn't been in love with him back then...*or*

had she? It was a question she always shied away from. She didn't like looking back. Regrets were for people who weren't confident in their ability to make choices.

She had made her choice.

She had chosen her career over marriage.

Not because she couldn't have combined them both, but more because Cristiano wouldn't have wanted her to. He'd wanted her to have babies and stay at home to rear them as his mother had done for him and his brother. He hadn't wanted any talk of nannies or childcare. In his opinion, there was only one way to bring up a family and that was to have a wife and full-time mother running the household.

They had argued about it constantly. For a while, Alice had naively thought he was only doing it to get a rise out of her. That he didn't really think so strongly about the issue but enjoyed the way she reacted when he expressed his opinion. But when he'd dropped that proposal on her, she'd realised he was deadly serious about it. For him there was no middle ground.

Marriage or nothing.

Alice had chosen nothing. Which had been fine when she was twenty-one with her whole life ahead of her. Now, at twenty-eight, with all her peers pairing up and marrying and starting families, and her own biological clock developing a recent and rather annoying and persistent ticking, she wondered if 'nothing' was going to keep her satisfied...if she had ever been so.

They finished their meal without much further conversation. Alice tried a couple of times to talk to him about his hotel plans for London, but he seemed disinclined to talk about anything but the arrangements to do with their marriage next month. His single-minded focus was a little unnerving to say the least. She wondered if he had pulled the drawbridge up on his personal life because she had got him to talk about his childhood in a way he had never done before.

When he led her out of the restaurant she half expected him to suggest they continue the evening by taking her somewhere else for a nightcap or coffee. But he simply drove her home and barely lingered long enough to walk her to the door.

Alice stood in the frame of her front door and watched the red glow of his taillights disappear into the distance. She flatly refused to admit she was disappointed. But when she went inside and closed the door, her beautiful house with its spacious rooms and gorgeous décor had never felt so empty.

CHAPTER FOUR

THE MEETING WITH the lawyer to deal with the prenuptial agreements was held the following day. Cristiano had organised to pick Alice up from the salon but she got held up with a client who had turned up late to her appointment, so when Alice came out to Reception she found Meghan talking to Cristiano, who had been kept waiting for nigh on twenty minutes.

Meghan turned around with a beaming smile. 'Congratulations! Oh, my God, it's so romantic. It's all over social media—everyone's tweeting about it. I knew there was something cooking between you two. I just knew it. You're engaged!'

Alice had never considered herself a consummate actor, but right then and there she thought she was worthy of an Oscar *and* an Emmy.

She moved closer to Cristiano and slipped an arm around his lean waist. 'Thanks. Yes, it is exciting. We're very happy.'

His arm came around hers, his hand coming to rest on the curve of her hip, the heat of his broad palm sending a red-hot current straight to her core. 'Aren't you going to kiss me hello?' he said, smiling down at her.

Alice smiled back through mentally gritted teeth.

'Not in front of my staff. You know how I am about public displays of affection.'

'Oh, I don't mind,' Meghan said, with her hands clasped in front of her as if waiting for the penultimate kiss scene in a romantic movie.

Alice eased out of Cristiano's hold to collect her bag from behind the counter. 'I'll be out for a couple of hours,' she said to Meghan. 'I've called in Suze to help with my Saturday clients while I'm away on the weekend.'

'I'm so happy for you both,' Meghan said. 'Can I do your wedding make-up? Please, please, please? Or are you going to do it yourself?'

'Erm…we're not having that sort of wedding,' Alice said. 'We're going to do things simply—'

'Not have a proper wedding?' Meghan's pretty young face fell as if all her facial muscles had been severed. 'But you *love* weddings. You put so much time and effort into getting your brides ready. You're the best at it in the business. Everyone says so. Why wouldn't you want to be a bride your—?'

'Because I just want to be married without all the fuss,' Alice said before her young employee let slip about the bridal magazines under the counter. Yes, she had two stashes of them—one for clients and one for herself. 'Besides, we're being married next month. There's no time to do anything extravagant. Cristiano's in a hurry, aren't you, darling?'

Cristiano's glinting black gaze left no room for doubt on the subject. 'I've been waiting seven long years to have you back where I want you. I don't want to waste a second more than I have to.'

'Show me your ring!' Meghan said.

Alice took it out of the pocket of her uniform and slipped it back on her finger. 'It's a little loose but—'

'Oh…' Meghan's expression failed to conceal her disappointment. 'It's very…erm…nice.'

'It's not the official one,' Cristiano said. 'That's being designed as we speak.'

'Oh, how wonderful.' Meghan's face brightened as if a dimmer switch had been turned to full beam. 'Alice loves a good engagement ring, don't you, Alice?'

Alice wanted to slip between the polished floorboards of her salon. Why hadn't she been a little more circumspect when examining her clients' engagement rings? She had oohed and aahed over so many beautiful rings. It was the classical settings she loved the most. Simple and elegant instead of big and flashy. She stretched her mouth into a smile. 'Sure do.'

After Meghan's next client came in, Cristiano put a hand beneath Alice's elbow and led her out of the salon. 'Nice kid.'

'Yes…'

And I'm going to make her drink boiling-hot wax when I get back.

'She's very enthusiastic.'

'I should probably warn you there will be paparazzi hanging—uh oh, too late.' His hand on her elbow shifted to go around her waist when a cluster of people with cameras and recording devices surged towards them. 'Let me handle it.'

Alice stood in the circle of his arm and listened to him give a brief interview about their whirlwind romance. He was scarily good at lying. No one would ever think he wasn't in love with her. What her mother was going to say about their engagement was something that was niggling at Alice's conscience. She hadn't yet called her to give her the heads up. She'd been delaying it because she had been so preachy about her mother's multiple marriages. She hadn't attended the last one on principle. How was her mother going to react to this news?

'We'd like to hear a comment from the blushing bride,' a female journalist said, pushing the recording device towards Alice. 'Your reputation as the go-to girl for wedding make-up is on the up and up. Does this mean you'll expand the business into Italy and beyond or will you be keen to start a family?'

Alice blithely ignored the slight pressure increase from Cristiano's fingers and painted on a bright smile. Why should she let him answer for her? She wasn't a ventriloquist's puppet. He might have cornered her in private, but in public, well, that was where she could win a few points back. 'We're going to get started on the baby-making right away, aren't we, darling?'

His eyes sent her a warning. 'I'd like a little bit of time with you all to myself first.'

After the press moved on, Cristiano took her firmly by the hand and led her down the street. 'What the hell were you playing at?'

Alice threw him a glance that could have cut through plate glass. 'Why do women get asked such ridiculous questions? Why didn't that journalist ask you if you were going to give up your career to start a family? Why are women always expected to give up everything they've worked so hard for?'

His mouth was pulled tight. 'I'm not asking you to have a child, for God's sake, Alice. All I'm asking is for six months of your time.'

'I can't believe women still have to put up with this crap,' Alice said. 'It's no one's business but mine if I want a baby.'

'Presumably it would also be your partner's business.'

Alice sent him a sideways glance but his expression gave little away. 'Do you plan on having a family with… with someone else after we're—?'

'No.'

'But you were so keen—'

'It's not something I envisage for myself now.'

Why? Because I ruined your dream of happy families?

Alice didn't like the feeling she'd been the one to change his mind. He would make a wonderful father. Why would he give up that dream of having a family of his own? He had so much to offer a child. Stability. Security. Love. She stopped walking and glanced at him again. 'Did I make you change your mind?'

His eyes met hers for a brief moment before he looked away and continued walking in long purposeful strides. 'We're going to be late for the lawyer if we don't step on it.'

Alice blew out a breath and trotted alongside him. 'I'm a career woman. So shoot me.'

A career woman with a vague sense of something missing…

Cristiano led her into the lawyer's office where they dealt with the business of signing the prenuptial agreements. It was all so cold and clinical it made Alice feel uncomfortable, as if she was breaking some sort of taboo. What about, *What's yours is mine and what's mine is yours*? It was contrary of her to be feeling so piqued because she had her own financial interests to protect, but still it made her wonder, if she had married Cristiano seven years ago, whether he would have insisted on drawing up such a clinical agreement.

The lawyer brought their meeting to a close with the news that a lump sum as promised in the will would be deposited in Alice's bank account now her engagement to Cristiano was official. The money did not have to be refunded if the engagement came to an end as in the marriage not taking place, which was a surprising footnote to Alice.

It was a large sum of money, enough to pay a decent deposit on new premises plus some, if not half, of the mortgage. She found it hard to understand why Volante Marchetti had stipulated that particular clause. Or had his grandmother known Alice would think twice about walking away with such a large amount of money without seeing the whole arrangement through?

When they were leaving the lawyer's office Alice got a call from her mother. She looked at the caller ID and grimaced. 'Hi, Mum, I was about to call you—'

'Tell me I'm dreaming,' her mother said loud enough for Cristiano to hear. Possibly the whole street. 'My daughter—the daughter who swore she would never ever get married—is now getting *married*?'

Alice turned away from Cristiano's satirical expression. 'Yes, it's all happened very quickly and—'

'See?' Her mother sounded smug. 'I told you love hits you out of the blue. When you meet the right one you just know. When's the wedding? I'll have to get something flash to wear. Will you be able to help me pay for something? I don't want to look frumpish. But for God's sake don't invite your father. You'll have to get someone else to walk you down the aisle. Not that he's been a proper father to you anyway, running off with that woman when you were barely out of nappies and carrying on about paying maintenance for all those years. Why you have to have a relationship with him now after all those years of no contact, I will never know. I won't go if he's there.'

'Mum, there's not going to be a big wedding,' Alice said, mentally rolling her eyes at her mother's usual tirade about her father. Twenty-six years was a long time to be bitter, especially as her dad hadn't had an easy time of it since, bringing up a disabled child with his most recent partner. 'We're having a low-key ceremony. We don't want a lot of guests. We just want to keep things simple to make it more...meaningful.'

'Oh, well, if you're too ashamed to have your own mother at your wedding then so be it,' her mother said in a wounded tone. 'I know I'm not posh like some of your precious clients, but I'm the one who brought you into the world and made every sacrifice I could to give you a decent childhood.'

A decent childhood?

Alice wanted to scream in frustration. Nothing about her childhood had been decent. Her mother was the type of woman who didn't feel complete without a man in her life. *Any* man. It didn't matter how bad he was, as long as he fulfilled the role of male partner. During her childhood Alice hadn't known who would be at their flat when she got home from school. There had been a revolving door on her mother's bedroom in her quest to find 'The One'.

There had been numerous partners over the years,

two of whom subsequently became husbands. The second husband after Alice's father had been a financial control freak and heavy drinker who used his fists and filthy tongue when he didn't get his own way. The third had made a pass at Alice the day her mother introduced her to him, and stolen money from her purse on two other occasions. Alice refused on principle to attend their wedding as a result. And since the wedding, her mother had been subjected to constant put-downs and fault-finding, and such financial hardship she regularly called on Alice for handouts. But if ever Alice said anything about her mother's partner she would defend him as if he were Husband of the Year.

'Mum, I really can't talk now,' she said. 'I'll call you when I get back from my...holiday.' She hung up and slipped her phone back in her bag.

Cristiano was looking at her with a thoughtful expression. 'You okay?'

Alice relaxed her stiff frown but she could see he wasn't fooled for a second. She blew out a breath. 'My mother and I don't agree on some things...lots of things, actually.'

'She didn't ask to meet me?'

Alice gave him a wry twist of her mouth. 'As long as you're male you tick the box as far as she is concerned.'

His frown formed a crevasse between his dark eyes. 'But you're her only child. Why wouldn't she insist on meeting the man who's going to be your husband?'

'She's not the overprotective type. Anyway, I'm an adult. I'm old enough to make my own decisions.'

'Did you tell her about us when you came back from Italy after we broke up?'

Alice thought back to that time, how angry she had

been, and how that anger, once she had cooled down, had turned to a deeper hurt. But her mother had been in the process of separating from her second husband who had found another partner—a woman only a year older than Alice.

Alice had spent hours and hours listening to her mother lament the loss of another marriage—how she was losing the love of her life and how she wouldn't be able to survive without him, *blah, blah, blah*. Alice had suppressed her feelings about her own breakup and channelled her energies into getting her mother through the divorce process, and then on starting up her own beauty business. There hadn't been time to examine too closely how she felt about Cristiano.

Maybe that had been a mistake...

'We don't have that sort of relationship,' Alice said. 'Not all mothers and daughters are best friends.'

'What about your father? Do you ever see him?'

'I didn't use to,' Alice said. 'But he tracked me down a couple of years ago. We meet up occasionally. Mostly when he needs money.'

Why did you tell him that?

His frown deepened. 'You don't give it to him, do you?'

Alice didn't want to go into the complex details of her relationship with her father. Charles *call-me-Chas* Piper was a happy-go-lucky charmer who, in spite of everything he had done and not done as a father, she couldn't help feeling a little sorry for. He was a hobby gambler and a regular drinker, but to his credit—after years of abandoning partners once he got bored—he had stayed with the young woman he'd married a few years ago. They had a son with severe autism and money was always tight on getting little Sam the support and care he needed.

Alice was a soft touch when it came to people with special needs. She told herself the money she gave to her father was for Sam, even though deep down she knew some of it would be spent on other things. But she figured her father and his partner Tania surely deserved something for themselves after everything they had been through. 'He's my father. He's not a bad person—just an unlucky one.'

'Unlucky in what way?'

Alice shook her hair back and readjusted the strap of her bag over her shoulder. 'Are we done? I have to get back to work. I have back-to-back clients this afternoon.'

Cristiano held her gaze for a long moment. 'I'll be around tonight. I'll bring dinner.'

Alice sent him a reproachful look. 'Here's a lesson in manners for you. What you say is: Would you be free this evening? I would like to bring you dinner. See? Not that hard, is it?'

He ran a lazy hand down the length of her arm. She was wearing a cashmere-blend cardigan over her uniform but still every nerve stood up and took notice, especially when he encountered her hand. His fingers closed around it and then he brought it up to his mouth. Alice watched in a state of mesmerisation when his lips brushed against the backs of her knuckles, his eyes holding hers in a lock that made something fall off a high shelf inside her stomach. The scrape of his stubble sent a shockwave of lust straight between her thighs. The clean sharp citrus scent of his aftershave teased her senses until she felt slightly drunk. She couldn't stop staring at his mouth—the shape of it was pure male perfection. Strong and firm, and yet with a sensual curve that could unravel her self-control in a hummingbird's heartbeat.

'Are you free this evening?' he said. 'I would like to bring you dinner.'

Alice could have done with a bit of that self-control right about now. She knew saying yes would be saying yes to other things besides dinner. How long would she be able to resist that mouth? Those hands? That body? So far he hadn't kissed her. So far. But how long before he did? 'Yes, I'm free.' *Sucker.*

A smile lifted the edges of his mouth and he released her hand. 'I'll look forward to it.'

Cristiano walked back to his hotel after he left Alice at her salon. His mind ran back over their conversation. In the past she had told him a bit about her background but he hadn't realised—or been astute enough back then— to read between the lines. He had been quietly envious of her having both parents still living so hadn't been able to see how complicated her relationship was with both of her parents. Her mother sounded like a petulant child, and her father asking Alice for money now he was back in her life after years of no contact was nothing short of scandalous.

But one thing he did know was that kids—no matter how difficult they were—loved their parents. It was a fact of nature. Bonds were created in childhood and it took a lot to destroy them.

Alice had been adamant about not marrying. She had voiced her opinions on the subject volubly. Heatedly. Stridently. He had—naively, perhaps—thought she was only saying it because she hadn't wanted to come across as a gold-digger. He was well aware of how his wealth made him an attractive prospect for a woman who was looking for security. That was another fact of nature. Women had good reason to want to connect with a man who could provide for her once it came time to have children.

But Alice insisted she didn't want children. That was another thing he didn't take all that seriously back then. What young woman of twenty-one wanted children at that stage of their lives? He'd been confident—too confident—she would change her mind once they were married.

Cristiano had been too proud to go after her when she'd rejected his proposal. Proud and angry. Bitterly, blindingly angry. He'd expected her to come crawling back. That was another thing he'd been far too confident about. He'd thought she'd go home and think about what she was throwing away and call him and say she'd changed her mind. But the only thing she'd changed was her phone number.

That was the nail that finally closed the lid on his hopes.

But now he wondered what was really behind Alice's adamant stance on marriage. Lots of kids of divorced parents went on to have successful marriages themselves. Was it because she was a staunchly independent career woman? Having a career didn't mean you had to give up everything else. Did she still hold those views or had she shifted some ground over the passage of time?

Her friendly little employee gave the impression Alice was a big fan of weddings. Word on the street was she was the go-to girl for bridal make-up. Did that mean she secretly dreamed of a white wedding with all the trimmings? But she hadn't dated anyone seriously in years. That was another thing he'd found out from her loquacious little workmate. Alice virtually lived and breathed work. She had no social life to speak of and always made excuses when friends tried to hook her up with potential dates.

He didn't want to admit how pleased he was about that. If he hadn't been happy for the last seven years then why the hell should she be? But then, she was a tetchy little thing. Not many men would put up with her quick temper and acid tongue. But behind that prickly exterior was a warm-hearted person. Some of the time.

Funny, but her sharp tongue had been one of the things he'd most admired about her back then. The fact she didn't kowtow to him because he was super rich. Losing his parents so young had made everyone—even his grandparents at times—tiptoe around him. No one ever said no to him or argued the point with him. He was so used to getting his own way he hadn't factored in anyone else's opinion on things until he'd met Alice. She never ran away from an argument or a difference of view. She didn't cave in to please him. She stood her ground and wouldn't budge if she believed she was in the right.

But what if she had changed? What if those rigidly held opinions on marriage and children had softened? *Too bad.*

Cristiano wasn't going down that road again. Family life was for people who could handle the risk of losing it in the blink of an eye. He had already lost one family. He wasn't going to sign up for a second.

His grandmother's machinations meant he had no choice but to jump through the hoops like an obedient circus dog, but that was as far as it would go. He had considered a register office ceremony but decided if he was going to get married then it would be the old-fashioned way. Besides, his *nonna* would come back to haunt him if he didn't repeat those wedding vows in front of a priest.

But you don't love Alice now.

Cristiano ignored the prod of his conscience. God would have to forgive him for borrowing His house of worship as a means to an end. Over the years he had downgraded his feelings. Told himself he hadn't loved Alice at all. It was too confronting, too painful to admit he had loved her and lost her. Instead he filed it away as nothing but a lust fest. A mad, once-in-a-lifetime passion that had taken him over like a raging fever. Consuming rational thought. Sideswiping common sense.

He was no longer that idealistic young man blinded by lust. He was older, wiser, harder. He could control his passion. He could control his desire. He could control his emotions.

A quiet church wedding with limited guests was the only way to go. There would be no chance of Alice misreading his motivations if he kept things clean and simple. And less complicated when it came time to end it.

For end it he would.

CHAPTER FIVE

ALICE TOLD HERSELF there was no reason she should be cleaning her house like someone with a serious case of obsessive-compulsive disorder but she wasn't going to have Cristiano counting the dust bunnies hiding under the sofa. She had never been able to justify employing someone to clean because she was hardly at home to make much of a mess.

Once she'd sorted the house, she got working on herself. That saying about plumbers with leaky taps equally applied to beauticians. When was the last time she'd waxed her legs? And as for a bikini wax…? It was so overgrown her 'lady land' looked as if Sleeping Beauty had taken up residence.

Well, come to think of it, maybe she had.

It had been about a hundred years since there had been any activity down there.

Alice reached for her perfume and spritzed her wrists and neck. This was probably a good time to ask herself why she was going to all this trouble.

You are so going to sleep with him.

She slammed the door on the thought. No. Not going to happen. She could resist him. Sure she could. He wasn't that irresistible.

Yikes. Yes, he was.

As long as he didn't kiss her it would be okay. Kissing him would be dangerous. Dangerous because his mouth had the amazing power to make her senses spin out of control like bald tyres on an oil spill.

The doorbell sounded and Alice jumped up and smoothed her skinny jeans down her thighs. She'd figured tight jeans might work as a reminder to her self-control. Not so easy to slip out of sprayed-on denim.

Then why did you put on your best bra and knickers?

Alice was getting a little annoyed with her conscience. Nice underwear was standard. So what if she'd put on her most expensive set? Her girls deserved the best support, didn't they? She opened the front door and tried not to swoon when she saw Cristiano standing there dressed in dark blue denim jeans and a crisp white casual shirt that was rolled up over his tanned forearms. His hair was still damp as if he had not long showered and his jaw was cleanly shaven. 'At least you're on time,' she said.

His gaze travelled over her slowly, smoulderingly, until she wondered if her clothes were going to be singed right off her body and left in a smoking heap on the floor at his feet. 'You look beautiful.'

Alice looked at his empty hands and then around him for any sign of the dinner he'd promised to bring. 'I thought you said you were bringing dinner with you?'

'It will be here soon.'

She stepped back and held the door open, breathing in a delectable whiff of his aftershave when he walked past. She closed the door and linked her hands in front of her body, more to keep them away from the temptation of touching him. 'I got the money,' she said. 'I checked my bank account an hour ago.'

'Good to know the lawyer is doing what he's been paid to do.'

Alice unhooked her hands and used one to tuck a strand of her hair back behind her ear. 'Any idea why your grandmother stipulated that clause? I mean, I could end our engagement right now and still be way out in front financially.'

'You could. But you won't.'

She frowned. 'What makes you so sure?'

He was standing close. So close she could see every individual pinpoint of his recently shaven jaw. So close she could feel the magnetic draw of his body. 'Because you're not the sort of girl who'd take money from an old lady without fulfilling the rest of the wishes she expressed.'

'But I hardly knew your grandmother. I only met her a couple of times. We chatted and all that but hardly long enough for her to want to include me in her last will and testament, I would've thought.'

'Maybe, but she liked you and you liked her.' He waited a beat. 'She saw something in you. A quality she warmed to.'

'Stubbornness?'

He gave a soft laugh. 'That and…other things.'

What other things? Alice wanted to ask.

'Would you like a drink? I have wine and soft drinks or—'

'Later.' He slipped a hand into the inside pocket of his dark blue blazer and took out a ring box from a designer jeweller. 'For you.' He flipped the box open and inside was a gorgeous diamond in a classic setting.

Alice took out the ring and watched as the light above their heads brought out the diamond's brilliance. It was so simple and yet so elegant. She slipped it over her finger and it sat there as if it had been made for her. 'It's…'

'If you say "nice" I will not be answerable for the consequences.'

Alice smiled and kept gazing at the ring. 'Perfect. It's perfect, that's what it is. It's exactly what I would have chosen.'

When she glanced up at him he was frowning. 'Would you have preferred that?' he asked. 'To choose it yourself?'

Alice had never seen him look so uncertain before. 'I guess if this was a normal situation then maybe I would have. But it's fine since it's not. Anyway, I'll give this back once we're done.'

'I don't want it back.'

'But it's—'

'It's yours, Alice. You can do what you want with it when we're through.' He released a short breath. 'I'm sorry. I should have consulted you on what you'd like. I didn't think. The old one was so…so inappropriate. I'm annoyed I didn't see that before. It didn't suit your hand at all.'

Alice shifted her lips from side to side. This was a new thing—Cristiano admitting to getting something wrong. 'Just your luck to pick someone so independent she can't even let a guy choose a ring for her.'

'It wasn't just the ring I got wrong, though, was it?'

Alice couldn't hold the sudden intensity of his gaze. She looked at the new ring instead and angled her hand so the light caught the facets of the diamond. 'Thing is, my mother has three rings, all of them ghastly. She pretended to love them when her partners gave them to her. I always wondered why she did that.' She glanced at him again. 'Surely if you're going to marry someone and agree to spend the rest of your life with them you'd be honest with them from the get-go?'

His mouth lifted in a rueful smile. 'That was another quality my grandmother liked in you. Honesty. You didn't filter your opinions. You spoke your mind and to hell with anyone who didn't agree with you.'

Alice couldn't help a tiny cringe at how outspoken she had been back then. She had been very much 'my way or the highway' in her thinking. She'd held strong opinions on issues that, in hindsight, she had not researched well enough to warrant holding such strident views. How many people must she have offended, or even hurt, by expressing such unqualified and often-times ignorant opinions? Back then she had considered the notion of compromise or backing down as a weakness, a flaw. But now…now she wondered if being able to give and take, and listen rather than speak, was a more mature and balanced way to approach life.

'I'm surprised your grandmother even remembered me. You and I were only together six weeks. There must've been a lot of women in your life since. I don't suppose she's left each of them—?'

'No. Just you.'

Alice wanted to ask if he had fallen in love with any of them but knew it would make him think she was jealous. Which to her great annoyance she was. It didn't seem fair that he'd moved on with his life so quickly when she had supposedly been his soul mate. What if she had changed her mind in the weeks after their breakup? Too bad, because he'd already partnered up with someone else.

'I know what you're thinking,' Cristiano said. 'You're thinking I didn't take long to replace you, yes?'

Alice hadn't realised her expression was so transparent. Or maybe he really could read her mind. Scary thought. 'You made no secret of your love-life. It was splashed over every gossip magazine.'

His gaze was unwavering. 'And that bothered you?'

Alice frowned. 'Why wouldn't it bother me? You bought me a frightfully expensive ring and told me I was the only woman in the world for you, and yet within a week or two of me ending our relationship, you're off with someone else.'

'Did you change your mind?'

'No, of course not.' Alice knew she had answered too quickly by the way one of his brows rose in an arc. 'I was just annoyed you hadn't...'

'Hadn't what?'

She let out a gusty little breath. 'Missed me.'

He stepped closer and placed his hands on the tops of her shoulders. 'You think I didn't miss you?'

Alice couldn't shift her gaze from his mouth. It was drawn there by a desire she could not override with self-discipline or common sense. The warmth of his hands was burning through her clothes, setting her skin on fire. Making her aware of his male body standing close—so close she could sense the stirring of his blood in tune with her own. She placed her hands flat against his chest, touching him, feeling the heat and strength of him.

Wanting him.

The deep thud-pitty-thud of his heart beneath her

palm reverberated through her body, sounding an erotic echo deep in the centre of her being. She curled her fingers into the fabric of his shirt, not caring that it caused it to crumple and the tiny buttons to strain against the buttonholes. She closed the hair's breadth distance between their bodies, an electric frisson coursing through her at the intimate contact.

What did it matter if she was the one to cave in first? It was what she wanted. What they both wanted. She had missed touching him.

Being held.

Being wanted.

Alice stepped up on tiptoe and pressed a barely touching kiss to the side of his mouth, her lips tingling from the contact with his newly shaven skin. Cristiano's minty fresh breath mingled with hers but he didn't take over the kiss. Was he trying to prove how strong he was compared to her? That he could resist her even if she couldn't resist him? She smiled to herself. She knew just how to get him to weaken. She sent the tip of her tongue out and licked the surface of his bottom lip. A cat-like lick to remind him of how clever she was with her tongue. How she had made him collapse at the knees when she got to work on him.

His hands went from her shoulders to her hips, tugging her so close she could feel the hardened, pulsing ridge of him against her belly. 'Haven't you heard that saying about playing with fire?'

Alice shamelessly stoked the fire by rubbing her pelvis in a circular motion against his. 'You want me.'

'I didn't say I didn't.'

'But you said our marriage won't be—'

'So, that rankled, did it?' A teasing glint danced in his eyes. 'I thought it might.'

So he'd said that deliberately to get a rise out of her? Did he want her or not? Or was he just playing with her? Letting her dangle like a pathetic mouse being tortured by a mean-spirited cat. Alice pursed her lips and tried to pull back but his hands were clamped on her hips. 'Let me go.'

'Is that really what you want?'

'Yes.' She all but spat the word out. But inside her body was screaming. *No-o-o-o!*

'Fine.' He dropped his hands and stepped away, a knowing smile lifting the edges of his mouth. 'No harm done, *si*? But if you change your mind, you know where to find me.'

Alice ground her teeth so hard she thought her molars were going to crack. The only harm done was to her pride. Why had she allowed him to get the upper hand? He'd fooled her into thinking he had changed. He had even expressed his regret—albeit in veiled terms—about the ring he'd bought in the past. But at the heart of it all he wanted to prove was he had moved on from her—that he hadn't got any lingering feelings where she was concerned. He hadn't missed her one little bit. He'd soon found someone else to scratch his itch. He might still desire her, but that was all he wanted from her now. Sex.

How different from what he had offered her in the past. Back then he'd promised her the world—his heart, his soul, his love. Now all he promised was mind-blowing, body-tingling sex. A trashy little affair to pass the time until they could end their relationship once they'd fulfilled the terms of his grandmother's will. How could she agree to something like that when it was so unlike what they'd had before?

Because you still want him, that's why.

Not that much.

Are you sure about that?

Alice wasn't so sure about a lot of things any more. The desire Cristiano stirred in her refused to bank down in spite of all her efforts to control her response to him. It was like simmering coals deep in her body, just waiting to erupt into leaping, quick-licking flames. Could she risk an affair with him and to hell with the consequences? She could keep her feelings separate. That was what men did without any bother. Why couldn't she?

'I'm not going to let you play games with me, Cristiano.'

'Games, *cara*?' His brow rose above one eye. 'Isn't that your specialty?'

Alice pressed her lips together. 'You won't win this. You think you can get me to beg? Think again. I don't want you anything like the way you want me.'

A satirical light entered his gaze. 'There's one simple way to test that little theory of yours. Would you like to try it?'

Alice stepped two more steps back and folded her arms across her body. 'If you come any closer I'll... I'll bite you.'

'Promise?' His sexy half-smile made something deep in her belly turn over.

The doorbell sounded and Cristiano reached past her to answer it. 'That will be our dinner.'

Cristiano carried the meal he'd organised to be delivered from a nearby restaurant through to where Alice had set up the dining table. She was angry with him for not acting on her invitation. He'd wanted to. So much his entire body throbbed with the need to crush his mouth to hers. Still throbbed. He wanted her but on his terms, not hers. What was she playing at anyway? A teasing kiss or two to prove he had no resistance when it came to her?

That he'd *missed* her?

He'd missed her all right. He'd missed her so damn much it had taken him months to sleep with another woman. The women he'd been seen in public with after their breakup were just casual dates, but he had not pursued them any further. A drink or two, a dance, a dinner or a show—that was all. He hadn't been able to stop himself comparing them to Alice. Finding fault with their looks, their clothes, their manners or their conversation—or lack of it. Even when he did start sleeping with partners, he'd felt something wasn't quite right. But he'd put that down to the fact of how different having a hook up or fling was from having a relationship where you truly got to know the person.

But had he known Alice? Truly known her? He hadn't even got her taste right in rings. Not that any ring would have been right given she looked upon marriage as a form of modern-day slavery.

Not that his views back then had helped. It had taken him a few more years than he was proud of to see where Alice had been coming from. His conservative views on marriage had undergone some significant changes. He no longer saw a woman's role in such black and white terms. He understood the need for women to have the opportunity to reach their potential career-wise in the way most men took for granted. Having both a career and a family was something as a young man he had never questioned, and yet for a woman it had so many more implications. Careers and children were hard to juggle if one wanted to do both things well. Even men these days were starting to question the high demands of corporate life and how it impacted on their relationships at home.

But while Cristiano might have changed some of his strong views, he wasn't so sure Alice had changed hers. She seemed even more committed to her career, with expansion plans on the horizon. She hardly ever dated, according to her helpful employee Meghan. Why was that? Alice was a normal healthy young woman in the prime of her life. Why wouldn't she be out there doing what every girl her age did? She didn't even have a housemate. She lived all alone in a gorgeous house that looked as if it could be in a beautiful homes magazine.

But was she happy?

Cristiano didn't think so…but then, maybe that was because he was annoyed she hadn't been as committed to him as he had been to her. Or was it more because she was seemingly happy and he wasn't? He hadn't been happy, not from the moment she'd told him they were over. How had he got it so screwed up? He'd thought she loved him. Her body had if not her heart. She had been his most giving lover, and without doubt the most exciting. He had blithely thought she would accept his proposal with unbounded enthusiasm.

Blithely or arrogantly?

He hadn't expected her to say no because back then he had been the one with the money and status. He was the Prize Catch as the press put it. He had chosen the restaurant that night in which to deliver his proposal, not out of design but eagerness. That was what annoyed him the most. He had been too impatient. He had picked the ring up on the way to meet her after work. That, too, had been more impulse than plan. He had walked past a high-end jeweller's and that had been it. Decision made. No thought had gone into it. It had simply *felt* like the right thing to do.

Which showed how much feelings weren't to be trusted. He had been so excited about his dreams for their future, so focussed on securing her commitment, that he hadn't picked up on her mood. He'd been like a goofy kid unable to contain himself. If he had waited until they got home to his villa in Milan would she have given him a different answer? If he had given her more time? A few days, weeks or even months? Would she have felt less pressured? Less cornered?

So what's changed?

Cristiano winced at the nudge of his conscience. He had cornered her again. Forced her to bend to his will. He had a goal to achieve. He was focussing on the big picture instead of examining the finer detail.

But he had to get those shares back before his cousin blew the lot. And he had to do whatever it took to keep the villa otherwise it would go to some stranger. He didn't have a choice any more than Alice did.

It was marry her or lose a third of his family's company and the villa he knew as home.

As if he were going to allow *that* to happen.

CHAPTER SIX

AFTER DINNER THAT night, Alice didn't see Cristiano again until Friday when he picked her up to take her to the airport for their flight to Italy. Being stressed from having to organise another beauty therapist to cover her for the weekend when her usual girl had to pull out at the last minute, as well as see her own clients and get away on time, hadn't done her mood any favours. She hadn't had time to refresh her make-up or send a brush through her hair. And God only knew what she'd thrown in her overnight bag this morning when she'd missed her alarm and had to pack in a frantic hurry. How dared Cristiano look so damn fresh and clean and smell so divine? Didn't he have to work and sweat like normal people?

Once they were seated on the plane in business class—*of course*—Alice leaned her head back against the headrest and closed her eyes. 'You would not believe the day I've had.'

Cristiano's hand came to rest on top of hers where it was lying on the armrest. 'Want to tell me about it?'

Alice looked at his hand on top of hers. His skin was so tanned and the sprinkle of dark hair so masculine compared to the smooth, pale skin of hers. His fingers curled around her hand, reminding her of the way his strong powerful body gathered her close in the past. His thumb began an idle stroking across the back of her hand, a mesmerising rhythm that stirred her blood. She disguised a little shiver...or at least hoped she did.

'First, I didn't hear my alarm. My phone was on silent last night because I— Well, anyway. Then I had a staffing issue, which is the bane of my life as a small business owner. Suze, the girl I'd organised to come in to do my Saturday clients, caught a stomach virus. To her credit, she was prepared to work but I can't expose my clients to illness. It wouldn't be fair to them if they caught it.'

Alice stopped to draw breath to find him looking at her with an unwavering gaze.

'Am I boring you?'

His lips curved upwards in a slow smile. 'Not a bit. Go on.'

Alice had trouble remembering what she'd been talking about. All she could think of was how delicious his mouth looked when he smiled. Not a mocking smile, but a smile that said: *You're fascinating to me.* His eyes too made her brain scramble. Intensely dark, fringed with thick black eyelashes her clients would have paid a fortune to graft on.

'Erm...so then I worked through my clients and two were late, which is a nightmare because it has a knock-on effect that makes me late for my next client and so on and so on. And then, my last client wanted to talk once I'd done her waxing. Her husband is unwell—he just got diagnosed with cancer. I could hardly rush her out the door, now could I?'

'Of course not.'

She let out a long exhausted-sounding breath. 'Beauty therapists are like hairdressers. No wonder we're called therapists. Half the time I'm more of a psychologist than I am anything else.'

His hand picked up hers and turned it over, his thumb stroking the inside of her palm in a slow circular pattern that made every rigid muscle in her back soften like honey in a heatwave. 'You enjoy your work, though, don't you?'

Alice didn't even have to think about her answer. 'I love it. I love being able to make women—and it's mostly women, but I have male clients too—feel good about themselves. I like the skin-care element too. I've been able to help numerous clients with troubled skin. Nothing lifts self-esteem more than feeling good about how you look.'

'So how did the wedding arm of your business come about?'

Alice couldn't remember talking to anyone this much about her work other than her employees and a couple of girlfriends. Her mother never showed much interest—she was always too worked up about her own issues and only required Alice to listen, not talk.

'Sort of by accident or serendipity. I did the make-up for a bride about five years ago, and then her bridesmaid chose me, and then she told her friends, and everything built up from there. Word of mouth still rules in spite of the digital age.'

Cristiano's thumb was on her pulse now, that same slow stroking motion on the underside of her wrist making her sink even further into the plush leather seat. 'So tell me about your expansion plans.'

'Well…my salon in Chelsea is getting too small

when I do weddings as well as normal clients,' Alice said. 'My regular clients aren't too happy if I book the salon out too many Saturdays in a row for weddings. I have a dream to set up a luxury wedding spa where brides and the wedding party can be the focus of attention. There will be an area for official photos or glamour shoots too. Of course I'll have to move between both salons at first, but ultimately I'd like to concentrate on the wedding side of things.'

'Because you have a thing about weddings?'

Alice gave him a beady look. 'The *money*. Weddings bring in the money, especially high-profile ones.'

His thumb stroked the fleshy pad of hers, making her legs feel as if someone had removed all the bones. 'You don't find it slightly…ironic?'

'Ironic I want to make money?'

He smiled a crooked smile. 'You know what I mean, Alice.'

Aleece.

Oh, dear Lord, how was she supposed to stay sane when he said her name like that?

She gave a little shrug. 'Just because I do a lot of bridal make-up doesn't mean I want to be one myself. You own and operate hotels, does that mean you want to live in one?'

His eyes didn't once leave hers. 'Not all marriages are slave camps. When a good marriage works it can be a wonderful thing.'

Alice gave him a pointed look. 'If you think it's so wonderful then why aren't you married by now?'

His thumb traced over the diamond on her left hand, his eyes still locked on hers. 'If all goes to plan I soon will be.'

Alice concealed a little swallow. 'But it's not like ours is going to be a normal one.'

'It could be if that's what you want.'

She frowned. 'You mean…last for ever?'

'No.'

Did he have to sound so damned emphatic?

'I meant we could have our fun while it lasts.'

Not for ever? Just 'fun' for now. Alice shifted her lips from side to side. 'If I agreed to…to having fun with you, does that mean you'll be having fun with other people at the same time?'

His mouth tilted in another smile. 'From what I remember of the fun we had together, I don't think I'd have the energy for anyone else.'

Alice held his gaze for a long moment. Was this wise? Offering to have an affair with him for the short duration of their engagement and marriage? What kind of arrangement was that? And could she trust him to remain faithful?

Funny, but she felt she could. He might have changed in other ways but she couldn't see him cheating on a partner. He wasn't that sort of man. 'Thing is… I haven't had a lot of fun just lately so you might be disappointed in what I bring to the…erm…game.' It seemed the right choice of word, all things considered.

Cristiano brought her hand up to his mouth, pressing his lips to the tops of her fingers, all the while holding her gaze with the steadiness of his. 'I can bring you up to speed in one session.'

I can well believe it. Alice tried but failed to suppress a frisson-like shiver. 'So…when would you want to…to start having fun?'

He slid a warm hand around the nape of her neck

and drew her inexorably closer, only stopping once her mouth was within a breath of his. 'I'd do you now but I wouldn't want to disturb the other passengers with your screams of pleasure.'

Alice kept her eyes trained on his smiling mouth, her heart leaping in excitement, her whole body trembling with feverish anticipation. Only he could make her sob with pleasure. Sob and scream and shudder from head to foot. How had she resisted him this long? It was crazy to keep denying herself the sensual thrill of his touch. So what if it only lasted a few months? A few months were better than no months. She'd spent the last seven years missing the magic of his lovemaking. Why not enjoy it while it lasted? 'You're not thinking of using one of the bathrooms?'

'No. I'm going to make you wait until we get home.'

Cruel. Cruel. Cruel.

Alice stroked a fingertip over his top lip, following the contours of his vermilion border, his stubble catching on her skin like a thorn on silk. 'I could take things into my own hands…' she said with a suggestive glance.

His eyes glinted and his hand on the back of her neck slid under the curtain of her hair, the slight drag on the roots sending a bolt of fizzing electricity down her spine. 'Hold that thought.'

Alice closed the distance between their mouths, touching hers down on his as softly as a butterfly landing on a petal. She eased back but because his lips were dryer than hers they clung to her softer skin as if they didn't want to let her go. He made a rough sound deep in his throat and brought his lips back to hers in a slow, drugging kiss that made her insides coil and twist and tighten with longing. His tongue entered her mouth in a smooth, deep glide that had a deliciously erotic element to it. It called hers into a sensual dance that made her feminine core contract with need. The kiss went deeper and deeper, drawing from her a response she had never given to anyone else. Shivers coursed through her body—her skin prickling, tingling, and aching for the touch of his hands. Her breasts suddenly felt too small for her bra—they were straining against their lace barrier, desperate to feel the warm, firm possession of his hands. To feel the stroke of his tongue, the hungry suckle of his lips, the sexy scrape of his teeth.

He shifted position, tilting her head to one side as he explored every secret corner of her mouth, the dark shadow of stubble around his mouth and on his chin abrading her softer skin like a fine-grade rasp.

Somehow the thought they were on a crowded plane and couldn't take the kiss any further only heightened the intensity of it. She couldn't remember kissing him in the past without it ending with them making love. Their first kiss had ended in bed. Every kiss of their affair had been the same. It was as if their lips couldn't touch without their bodies being engulfed by raging desire. They hadn't kissed in public other than a quick brush of the lips because she hadn't been comfortable about public displays of affection. Still wasn't, which made it all the more surprising—if not a little shocking—that she was doing it now, within sight and hearing of three hundred fellow passengers.

But every pulse-racing moment of it tantalised her senses until she completely forgot where they were. She spread her fingers through his thick black hair, greedily succouring his mouth as if without it she would die. She made a mewling sound in her throat, her need of him escalating. No one had ever kissed her like this. No one had ever made her feel this way. This madness, this ferocious need that clawed at her core and made every inch of her flesh scream and beg and plead for release.

Cristiano finally pulled back, his hands still cradling her face, his eyes so dark it was impossible to identify his pupils from his irises. He pressed the pad of his thumb to her kiss-swollen lower lip and then to a spot on the middle of her chin. 'I've given you stubble rash.'

Alice traced a fingertip around his mouth, the floor of her stomach giving a kick like a miniature pony when his masculine roughness caught at her skin. 'I'm running an autumn special on lip and chin waxes if you're interested.'

His eyes glinted their amusement. 'Thanks, but I'll pass.'

She stroked a fingertip down the bridge of his nose and then the shallow trench of his philtrum ridge down to where it met his top lip. His lips twitched as if her touch tickled. Then he captured her finger and closed his lips over it, drawing on it while his tongue stroked its underside, his gaze holding hers in a sensual lock that made her insides shudder.

How could it be possible to want any man more than she wanted this one? Was that why she had bolted when he'd pressured her to marry him in the past? Because he was the one man who could make her forget about her promise never to become enslaved to a man. Never to lose her autonomy. Never to need someone so badly they had the power to destroy her. Cristiano had the power to destroy her self-control. He only had to look at her and her self-control folded like a house of cards in a gale-force wind.

Cristiano took one of her hands and threaded his fingers through hers. 'I've been thinking… I don't remember ever kissing you before without it ending in sex.'

Alice ran her tongue over her lips, tasting him. Wanting him. Aching for him. 'I was thinking the same. Freaky, huh?'

His gaze searched hers for a long moment. A small frown tugged at his brow, making a two-pleat fold between his eyes. 'I seem to remember we didn't do a lot of talking back then, either.'

Alice gave him a wry look. 'I don't know about that. I talked but you didn't listen.'

His crooked smile had a faint touch of regret about it. 'We didn't listen to each other.' He released a long sigh and looked at their entwined fingers, his thumb rhythmically stroking the length of hers. 'It was a long time ago, *si*?'

Alice settled into the seat, resting her head against his shoulder. 'It sure was.'

So much so I feel like a different person now.

CHAPTER SEVEN

IT WAS CLOSE to midnight when they arrived at Cristiano's villa in Milan. Stepping over the threshold was like stepping back through time.

Alice swept her gaze around the stunning entry, taking in the marble floors and the grand staircase that led to the upper floors with its decorative black balustrading. There were priceless chandeliers and wall lights, the marble and bronze statues and artworks that would be the envy of any serious art collector. Some things were the same, and yet others were different. It had been redecorated and repainted but it was still Cristiano's home—the place where he had spent the first eleven years of his life until the tragic death of his family.

The villa had been rented out following his parents' and brother's deaths as Cristiano had lived in Stresa with his grandparents. But Alice knew how much this place meant to him. He had spent the happiest years of his life here.

She had spent the happiest six weeks of her life here.

Cristiano took her hand and drew her to his side. 'Having second thoughts?'

Alice turned in the circle of his arms and linked her arms around his neck. 'No. Why would I? It's just sex.'

His gaze held hers for a long beat. 'You're not worried about the boundaries blurring?'

Worried? Damn straight, I'm worried.

'No,' Alice said. 'But clearly you are. What are you worried about? That you might fall in love with me all over again?'

A steel shutter slammed down at the backs of his eyes. 'I told you before—I wasn't in love with you. I was in lust.' He dropped his hold and stepped away from her. 'I'll take the bags up. You go on ahead. I'll be up in a minute.'

Alice stood without moving. Did he have to make it sound so…so clinical? He was making her feel like someone he'd picked up in a bar and brought home for a quick tumble. Where was the man who had once carried her up those stairs like an old-time Hollywood-movie hero? Who had treated her like a princess instead of a prostitute?

'Are any of your household staff here?'

'No. I gave them the night off. I called them before we left London.'

Alice could sense he was annoyed with her. Every muscle in his face was pulled tight, especially around his mouth, leaving it flat and white-tipped.

'Why don't we go up together?' she said.

'You know where my bedroom is.'

Alice lifted her chin. 'Oh, I get it. You want to play I'm-the-John-and-you're-the-hooker? Fine—I can do that.'

She shrugged off her light coat and let it drop to the floor. Then she unzipped her dress and let it puddle at her feet before she stepped out of it, leaving her in bra and knickers and heels.

His eyes turned black, his mouth compressed until his lips disappeared. 'Don't.'

'Don't what?' Alice said, unhooking her bra and tossing it to the floor near his feet. 'I'm having fun, aren't you?'

He kicked her bra out of the way and came to her before she could remove anything else. He took her by the upper arms, his fingers gripping her so tightly she was sure they would leave marks. 'Why must you always fight me at every turn?' he said.

Alice glared back at him. 'I'll fight you until you start treating me as an equal.'

'Then start behaving like an adult instead of a child.'

She pushed her naked breasts against the hard wall of his chest. 'How's this for acting like a grown-up?' She slid her hand down between their bodies to touch his swollen length. 'And this?'

His mouth came crashing down on hers as if some formerly strong leash of self-control inside him had finally snapped. It wasn't a kiss of tenderness, of exploring and rediscovering, but a kiss of raw, rampant hunger.

Alice kissed him back with the same frantic need, their tongues duelling, fighting—a heated, potent combat that made her senses career out of control. She tore at his clothes, tugging off his shirt with no concern for the buttons. She barely registered the *plink*, *plink*, *plink* of them hitting the marble floor. Next she unhooked his belt and slipped it from his trouser lugs, letting it drop to the floor at their feet.

His hands shoved her knickers down past her thighs, his fingers stroking her damp heat with devastating expertise. The pleasure came at her from nowhere, ambushing her, throwing her into a whirling tailspin that left her gasping.

But no way was she allowing this to be a one-way affair. She ripped his zipper down and freed him into her hands, massaging him as she fed off his mouth, using her tongue against his to remind him of the sensual assault she had in mind for him. He made a guttural sound—a sound so utterly primal it made her insides quiver in excitement.

He wrenched her hand away with a muttered curse, his mouth coming back down on hers with a fireball of passion. He walked her backwards to the nearest wall, part walk, part stumble, and roughly stepped out of his trousers and shoes.

Alice broke the kiss to peel her knickers the rest of the way down her legs and kick off her heels. Cristiano tugged her by the hips back against him, letting her feel the full force of his arousal. Her hand went to him again, while her eyes met his. She loved watching the waves of pleasure contort his handsome features. It was the only time she had ever seen him lose control.

'Wait,' he said, breathing hard. 'Condom call.'

Alice would have thrown caution to one side like her clothes, but knew it would be irresponsible given their circumstances. Not that she didn't allow herself a tiny moment, while he sourced a condom from his wallet, to wonder what it would be like to carry his child.

Cristiano came back to her, one hand going to the wall next to her head, his mouth pressing a hot kiss to the side of her neck, and then over her collarbone and then to her breasts. His tongue stroked each upper curve before circling the nipple, in ever tightening circles until he took the nipple into his mouth, drawing on it in a sensual suck that made the hairs on Alice's head stand on end as if pulled from above.

He kissed his way back up to her mouth, taking it in a deep, plundering kiss that left her clawing at his body for the release she craved. He moved between her legs, lifting one of her legs up and anchoring it on his hip before entering her with a sure, swift thrust that made her gasp out loud.

It had been so long!

He set a fast rhythm as if he knew the sweet and savage agony her body was going through. He drove into her moist heat with determined purpose, his breathing just as ragged as hers. Alice gripped him by the shoulders, her fingers digging into his muscled flesh as the wave broke over her. A smashing wave that tossed her into a spinning whirlpool that shook and shuddered through her body. And then another and another followed in its wake, leaving her boneless, spent and quivering all over with aftershocks.

He continued to rock against her until he came with a deep groan of release, his body shuddering as it emptied, his breath hot and rapid against the side of her neck.

Alice unlocked her fingers and slid her hands down his arms and back up again. 'You certainly haven't lost your touch. But I guess you've had plenty of practice.'

He pulled away from her and removed the condom. Then he bent to pick up his trousers and stepped back into them. 'I'm not going to apologise for having a life.'

Alice stepped past him and scooped up his shirt and slipped her arms through the sleeves, drawing it around her naked body, figuring it was quicker than fumbling around the floor for her clothes, which seemed to be strewn from one end of the foyer to the other. 'Are you suggesting I haven't got one?'

He gave her a levelling look. 'You haven't dated in over a year. Why?'

Alice pursed her lips, locking her arms even tighter around her body where she was trying to hold his shirt in place. 'I've been busy at work. I'm always too exhausted at the end of the day for trawling around the nightclubs or online for a sex buddy. Thanks to your extremely generous grandmother, I can now indulge myself for the next six months with you. Lucky me.'

A line of tension pulled at his mouth. 'Is that all you want from men? Sex?'

'Not all men,' Alice said. 'Only the ones I can bring myself to sleep with.' She stepped forwards and trailed a fingertip down his bare arm. 'You tick all the boxes. You're rich, good-looking and you know your way around a woman's body. Oh, and you always have a condom handy. That's always a bonus.'

His hand capturing her wrist, he searched her gaze for a long pulsing moment. 'You're twenty-eight years old. Don't you want more for your life now than work and no-strings sex?'

Alice closed her mind to the image it kept throwing up of a tiny dark-haired baby with raisin-black eyes. 'Nope. Do you?'

Cristiano's frown made a roadmap of lines on his forehead. His hand fell away from her arm. 'No.'

Alice bent down and picked up her bra and knickers and bundled them into a ball in her hand. 'Then we've got nothing to worry about, have we? We're both in this for what we can get. You want your company shares and your share of the villa and I want the financial security my share in your grandmother's villa will give me once we fulfil the terms of her will.' She slipped on her heels before adding, 'Although, I'm not sure why you're insisting on having a church wedding. It seems a little over the top given the circumstances.'

'I told you my reasons. I don't want people thinking this is anything but a genuine relationship.'

'All the same, it's going to look pretty bad when we divorce in six months,' Alice said. 'Aren't people going to speculate and wonder how genuine it was then?'

He gave her an unreadable look. 'Perhaps you won't want it to end in six months. You might be enjoying yourself too much.'

Alice laughed. 'Funny man. You're good in bed, but not *that* good.'

He sent a lazy fingertip over the back of her hand where it was holding his shirt in place. 'Speaking of bed… I hope I didn't rush you just then?'

'Did you hear me complaining?'

A small smile lifted one corner of his mouth. He sent the same fingertip down the slope of her cheek, stopping beneath her chin to lift it so her gaze was on a level with his. 'I want you like I've wanted no other woman.'

Alice gave up trying to hold his shirt together and linked her arms around his waist instead. 'I bet you say that to every woman you've brought back here.'

He made a twisted movement of his mouth. 'You might not believe this, but I've never brought anyone back here. For a drink or dinner, yes, but not to have sex. Not since you.'

Alice did find it hard to believe. But why hadn't he brought anyone back here? Did it mean he had loved her after all? That he couldn't bear to have anyone here where he had made such passionate love to her? But he was so adamant now he hadn't been in love with her back then. 'But why not?'

His eyes dipped to her mouth but whether it was because he was thinking of kissing her again or avoiding her gaze she couldn't be sure. 'Every room reminded me of you.' He waited a beat before returning his eyes to hers. 'It was…off-putting.'

'It must have cost you a fortune in hotels,' Alice said.

His crooked smile made her insides shift. 'The upside of owning hotels is I don't get to pay for accommodation.'

'Lucky you.'

His hands went to her hips, holding her against the stiffening of his body. The sensation of him swelling against her stirred her blood, making her aware of the tingling nerve endings deep in her core. His mouth came down and covered hers in a long, slow kiss that ramped up her desire to a new level.

Alice returned his kiss, her tongue tangling with his in a sexy tango that made him tug her harder against him as if he couldn't bear to have any distance between them. She moved her hands up and down his back and shoulders, delighting in the freedom to touch him, to stroke him, to feel his sculpted muscles tense and flex under her caressing touch.

She couldn't get it out of her mind—he hadn't brought anyone back here since her. Not one woman. No one had shared his bed with him but her.

Cristiano's hands went from her hips to scoop her up in his arms. 'Time for bed?'

Alice played with the ends of his hair that brushed

his neck. 'You don't have to carry me. I'm too heavy. You'll herniate a disc or something.'

He pressed a brief hard kiss to her lips. 'You're a lightweight. I lift weights that weigh more than you.'

He had the muscles to prove it. She could feel them bunching and tensing under her knees and her back where his arms were holding her, a heady reminder of how strong he was and how potently male.

He took her to his bedroom, which had been re-decorated since she had last been there. Had he tried to remove every memory of his time with her? Tried and failed? It was now decorated in a soft mushroom grey on a feature wall behind the bedhead, with white walls and ceiling, and white linen on the king-sized bed with a matching grey throw placed neatly on the end. There was a grey velvet linen-box-like seat at the foot of the bed half the height of the mattress. The carpet was a soft cream that threatened to swallow her up to the knees when Cristiano placed her on her feet beside the bed.

Alice kept her arms linked around his neck, pushing her body against the warm, hard frame of his. 'You've redecorated since I was last in here.'

'Yes.' He nibbled at her earlobe, sending a frisson scooting down her spine. 'Not that it worked. I still couldn't bring myself to make love with anyone in here. I spent a veritable fortune for nothing. Like it?'

'It's gorgeous.'

'Like you.' He kept kissing her neck, nipping and licking at the sensitive flesh.

Alice couldn't help a thrill of pleasure at his compliment. She didn't see beauty when she looked in the mirror. What woman did? She only saw the things she wished she could change. But when Cristiano looked at her with his dark eyes glittering with desire, she felt beautiful and desirable in a way she never felt with anyone else.

His mouth came to hers in a searing kiss, his tongue delving between her lips in search of hers. She gave herself up to the kiss, a soft whimper escaping her lips when he peeled his shirt away from her body and took possession of one of her breasts in his hand. The warm expertise of his touch made her skin tingle and her nipples tighten into buds. He rolled his thumb over her nipple, his hand then slipping to the underside of her breast, pushing the globe of flesh upwards for the descent of his mouth. He suckled on her engorged nipples in turn, his tongue hot and moist as it moved over the curve of each breast until her body was trembling with need.

He knelt down in front of her, kissing his way from her breasts, down her sternum and to her belly button. He lingered over the tiny cave, dipping the tip of his tongue into its whorled pool before going lower. Alice sucked in a sharp breath as his tongue skated over her lower abdomen, his warm breath a tantalising caress on her most intimate flesh. He separated her folds with his fingers and then brought his mouth to her, making every swollen nerve ending vibrate with delight. The spiralling waves of sensation pulsed through her body with earth-rocking force.

She tried to hold onto her consciousness but it was impossible to do anything but feel. Aftershocks of pleasure rang through her flesh, like a bell reverberating long after it had been struck.

Cristiano got up and eased her down on the bed, only stopping long enough to dispense with his trousers and access another condom. Alice reached for him as he came down over her on the mattress, her hands running over his muscled biceps and then the back of his neck, lifting her head to meet the descent of his mouth.

His kiss was long and deep, thrumming with a building urgency she could feel in every cell of her flesh where it was touching his. His erection probed her entrance and she opened to him, shifting her hips to accommodate him. It was like resuming a dance choreographed just for them. The fit of their bodies in that intimate embrace felt so right, so fluid and sensual—as unconscious and natural as breathing.

Alice stroked his back from his neck to his lower spine, concentrating in the dip above his taut buttocks. She knew all his erogenous zones and it thrilled her to feel his earthy response to her touch. She cupped his buttocks, holding him, rocking with him as he set a rhythm that was in perfect tune with her needs. The feel of him moving inside her body sent her senses into a frenzy of excitement.

No one filled her the way he did. No one knew her body as he did. No one else understood how much she craved this magic of motion, the friction that ruthlessly teased her sensitive flesh until she thought she would explode.

He turned her over so she was on top, his hands cupping her breasts, his dark gaze consuming her as a starving man did a meal he had long waited for in frustrated agony. Alice bent forward over him, her hands placed either side of his head, her hair falling forward to tickle his chest and shoulders. She moved her body in time with his, finding the extra friction that sent her over the edge. The savage pleasure pulsed through her in ever expanding waves like a boulder dropped in a pond. Every part of her body felt the rippling flow of release, until finally a warm soothing tide of lassitude was left in its wake.

His release was close behind hers, the spasms so powerful she could feel them echoing against the walls of her intimate flesh. She could see, too, the contortion of ecstasy played out on his face, and hear his sexy, breathless grunts that made her skin lift in a shower of goose bumps.

Cristiano rolled her back under him, and, balancing his weight on his elbows, he brushed the damp tendrils of hair back off her forehead. 'You never fail to surprise me.'

Alice teased the curls at the back of his neck with her fingers. 'In what way?'

He outlined her mouth with a lazy fingertip, the top lip and then the bottom one until her lips were tingling, his eyes sexily hooded. 'You respond to me like no one else.'

Alice didn't want to be reminded of all the other women he had slept with since her. Even if he hadn't brought them back here, she knew he had slept with dozens of women elsewhere. All those hook-ups in his hotels. Night after night. Year after year. It was too painful to think about—especially while her body was still thrumming with the magic of his touch.

She knew it was inconsistent of her to be so petty about it since she'd been the one to end their relationship. But the thought of him making love to someone else with the same intensity was nothing short of torture. How many women? Had he looked at them the way he looked at her? Had he touched them the way he had touched her? Was he making comparisons? Finding her a disappointment now he'd revisited their intimacy?

She dropped her hands from his hair and began to push against his chest. 'You'd better take care of that condom before we end up with more than a six-month marriage.'

A frown brought his brows together, his eyes studying hers for a beat or two. But then he rolled away and got off the bed and dealt with the condom. He picked up a bathrobe from the hook behind the door and slipped his arms into it and loosely tied the ties. 'Are you on the pill?'

'Of course.'

He bent to pick up his trousers from the floor and hung them over the back of a chair near the window. His expression had gone back to neutral but Alice couldn't help feeling he was annoyed with her again. She could see it in the way he was restoring order to the room. It was his way of controlling his feelings. A battening down of the emotional hatches, so to speak. Funny, but she hadn't realised he did that until now.

She hugged her knees to her chest and rested her chin on top of them, watching him fold his shirt he'd taken from her body such a short time ago. 'You're angry.'

He tossed the shirt to one side as if it personally offended him, and frowned at her. 'What gives you that idea?'

Alice unlocked her arms from around her knees and got off the bed, taking the bed throw rug with her as a sarong. 'I'm going to take a shower while you play housemaid.'

His hand captured her arm on the way past and he turned her to face him. 'What do you mean by that?'

'You're cleaning up the room as if you want to forget what just happened.' Alice unpeeled his fingers one by one, shooting him a look. 'Of course I'm on the pill. Do you think I'd sleep with you if I wasn't?'

His eyes held hers in a lock. 'Even the pill isn't fool-proof. You could miss a dose or have an absorption problem.'

'True, so that's why we have to be careful.'

Even though every time I think about a baby my ovaries start jumping up and down in excitement.

His gaze continued to bore its way into hers. 'So you're as adamant as ever over not having kids?'

Alice hoped he couldn't hear her eggs jostling and shoving each other and saying, *Let me go first!*

'My business is my baby. It takes all my energy and commitment. I don't have room in my life for a child. Anyway, what's with the inquisition? You're not thinking of making an heir and spare to inherit your millions, are you?'

The skin around his mouth tightened until it was more white than tan. 'No.'

'That's quite a change from the man seven years ago who couldn't wait to start a family.'

'I have different goals now.'

'What did your grandmother think about that?'

Cristiano's expression turned rueful. 'She wasn't happy about it. She only had my father and would've loved more children but it never happened. She had a stillbirth before my father and numerous miscarriages after.' He let out a long slow breath and continued. 'She adored my mother. She treated her as if she were her own daughter. There was none of that mother-in-law angst everyone talks about. My mother loved Nonna as much if not more than her own mother. Family was everything to Nonna.'

Alice had seen that love of family first hand when she'd met Volante Marchetti. Even though the old woman had not long ago lost her husband Enzo, she had been nothing but warm and loving and welcoming towards Alice. And when it came to Cristiano, well, Alice had felt slightly envious to see the depth of love the old woman had for him. There were parents who didn't love their children more than Volante had loved her grandson. 'Why do you think she wanted you to marry me? Surely she must've known it was the last thing either of us would want?'

'I'm not sure...' He dragged a hand down his face, the sound of his palm scraping against his stubbly jaw loud in the silence. 'No, that's not quite true. She was unhappy with how I was living my life. She was quite vocal about it towards the end. She wanted the best for me, and, in her mind, didn't think I was getting it.'

Alice gave a soft little snort. 'I hardly think I'm the best thing that's ever come into your life.'

Cristiano's gaze met hers for a long beat of silence. 'Nonna would disagree.'

'That's very kind of her, but I'm—'

'It's fine, Alice,' he said. 'I'm not going to hold you to our agreement longer than necessary. I'm only allowing it to go this far because I can't allow those shares to get into my cousin Rocco's hands. I'm not going to watch everything my parents worked so hard for go down the mouth of a poker machine or on a gaming table.'

Alice frowned. 'Didn't your grandmother know about his gambling tendencies?'

He shook his head, his look grim. 'I made the decision not to tell her. Stupid, I know now in hindsight. But she was so ill and frail and I didn't want to send her to her grave with that worry on top of everything else. She changed her will a week or two after her diagnosis.'

'Would you have tried to stop her if you'd known at the time what she planned to do?'

He seemed to consider it for a moment. 'I'm not sure… Yes, no, maybe. It was what she wanted so what right did I have to try and change her mind? She wasn't suffering from dementia or any mental impairment brought on by her illness. She had a right to compose a will that reflected her dying wishes, and yet… I wish I'd warned her about Rocco, but, to be honest, I'm not sure I would have even if I'd known what she planned to do. She adored him. He's her late sister's only child and her godson. It would have broken her heart to know he wasn't the golden boy she believed him to be.'

Alice shifted her mouth from side to side, thinking about Volante Marchetti with her razor-sharp mind and intelligent gaze. Not much would have escaped that wise old bird's eye. 'What if she did know?'

Cristiano looked at her blankly. 'Know what? About Rocco?'

'Yes. Maybe she knew you would do anything to save those shares from being frittered away,' Alice said. 'Anything, as in marrying your enemy.'

He gave her a sideways smile and glided a hand down the length of her bare arm, making her skin lift in a veil of goose bumps. 'Is that what we are? Enemies?'

Alice put her hand to his face, sliding it down the raspy skin of his cheek. 'Well, you could say we are, except now we're making love not war.'

He gathered her close, locking his hips against hers,

stirring her senses into overdrive with the heated probe of his body. 'I thought you were going to take a shower?'

She moved against him, her inner core leaping in excitement to find him hard as stone. 'I was. Want to join me?'

He unwrapped her from the throw, his eyes going to her breasts. He bent his head and covered one tightly budded nipple with his mouth, drawing on the puckered flesh until she was restless with clawing need. She worked on his trousers, unzipping them with more haste than finesse. His mouth came down on hers in a scorching kiss, his tongue tangling with hers in a tango of lust that made her blood all but sizzle in her veins. She could feel the swell of her most intimate flesh, the dragging sensation of need that was part pain, part pleasure. His hands gripped her by the hips, holding her to the pulsing heat of his body, his chest crushed against her breasts, the masculine hair tickling and teasing her sensitised skin.

Cristiano took her by the hand and led her to the en suite. He prepared himself with a condom while he waited for the shower to get to the right temperature, and then stepped in with her. The water cascaded over their bodies, heightening Alice's senses as his hands skimmed her wet, naked flesh. She pressed her lips to his chest, kissing her way down to his navel, circling her tongue and then bending down in front of him so she could take him in her mouth. She had never pleasured another partner this way. Had never wanted to. Had made excuses not to. The thought of doing it with someone else was almost repugnant. But with Cristiano it felt like a sacred act, one that was mutually pleasurable, for she loved feeling the potent strength of him against her lips and tongue. She loved hearing his groans, and witnessing his knees buckle when she drew on him. She loved feeling his hands gripping her head to anchor himself against the tumultuous throb of release.

But this time he wouldn't let her take him over the edge. He pulled away from her and brought her back to her feet. Then he bent down so he was between her parted thighs, his mouth working its magic on her feminine folds. He knew exactly what pressure and what speed to trigger the explosion. It rocked through her body like a torpedo, sending ripples of delight through every cell until her thighs tingled as if they were being trickled with fine sand.

Alice tugged him by the hair to get him to stand up, pressing her mouth to his and tasting her own essence on his lips and tongue. He moved from her mouth down to her neck, nudging and nuzzling her while he positioned himself. She guided him with her hand, lifting one leg so it was balanced on his hip, a gasp puffing out of her lips when he surged into her with his own raw groan.

The water falling over them added another sensory delight, the rocking speed of his thrusts ramping up her need until she was on the knife-edge, teetering there but unable to go any further. Cristiano pulled out and, with a sexy glint in his eyes, turned her so that her back was to him. Alice planted her hands on the marble wall of the shower, standing on tiptoes so he could gain the access he wanted.

There was something about this position that had an element of wickedness about it. A primitive wickedness that was as thrilling as it was slightly shocking. He moved between her buttocks, the hot glide of his engorged flesh tantalising her senses until she was breathing hard in excitement. He surged into her wetness, the different angle catching her right where she needed it, the fast-moving friction of his urgent thrusts triggering an orgasm so powerful she felt it move through her like a high-speed missile. The whirlpool of pleasure stole every conscious thought, leaving her spinning in a swirling black sea of magic.

Cristiano gave three more powerful thrusts, his legs quaking against hers, his breathing rough and uneven next to her ear. Alice waited for him to collect himself before she turned in his arms, locking her arms around his neck and pressing a lingering kiss to his mouth. His hands settled on her hips, his mouth moving against hers with slow, heart-tripping deliberation.

After a long moment, he lifted his head, his gaze dark, rich and gleaming with sexual satiation. 'Like old times, *si*?'

Alice licked her tongue over his lower lip, leaning into the hard warmth of his body. 'Better.'

Way, way better.

CHAPTER EIGHT

CRISTIANO WOKE NOT long before dawn to find Alice nestled up against his chest soundly asleep. Her hair was tickling his chin but he didn't have the heart to disturb her. Or maybe it was more because lying here with her was like time travelling back to a time in his life when he'd felt he had ticked all the boxes. Felt complete and satisfied in a way he hadn't since. One of her hands was resting against his chest, right over his heart. Her silken legs were entwined with his in an intimate linkage that made his blood stir.

Would this hunger for her ever be satisfied? How many times had they made love last night? He had been like a randy teenager. He couldn't seem to get enough of her. Was it a case of making up for lost time or... something else?

He didn't want to think about the something else.

He wasn't sure why he'd told Alice about his reluctance to sleep with anyone else here since her. Why should he care if she thought he'd bedded anything in a skirt for the last seven years? But somehow what they'd shared under this roof had meant something to him even if it hadn't to her. He hadn't wanted to dilute those memories with a host of other bodies, other faces, other smiles, and other perfumes. Or maybe it was a form of self-flagellation. A perpetual punishment for being so foolish to believe she had been The One.

No. He was fine with things as they were. What could be better than to make the most of their 'forced' time together? Wasn't that what he'd wanted? A chance to get her out of his system so he could finally move on with his life?

It was a good plan.

An excellent plan.

Why had his *nonna* orchestrated it other than to force him to revisit his relationship with Alice? His grandmother knew his life hadn't been the same since Alice left. She knew he hadn't moved on. Not properly. But to leave half of the Stresa villa to her seemed a bit of an extreme measure. Not that he'd let on to Alice how much the place meant to him. He'd let her think the company shares were his focus. The lakeside villa—like this one in Milan—had been in the Marchetti family for a hundred and fifty years. To lose one pebble, let alone half of the property, to someone outside the family was unthinkable. Even if it was to Alice, with whom he'd had the most passionate affair of his life.

There was nothing to stop her selling her share out from under him when their marriage ended. There was no guarantee she would give him first option. She might not even want to sell her share, which would mean he would have to sell his, or deal with having to share the villa with her on an ongoing basis. He could think of nothing worse than having to negotiate times to visit so he didn't run into her new lover or house-party guests. His family home reduced to a time-share property? Unbearable.

Alice's breathing was soft and even, but every now and again she would release a little purring sigh of contentment and nestle even closer. How many times had he watched her like this in the past? Dreaming of their future together, the life they would live, the children they would have, the happiness they would create together to make up for the tragedy he'd experienced.

He had her back in his bed, but would it be enough?

It would have to be because there was no way he was going to offer her anything else. His days of wearing his heart on his sleeve—or anywhere on his person, for that matter—were well and truly over. His heart was in lockdown. In solitary confinement. No walks in the exercise yard. No day release. No bail. No parole.

This thing between him and Alice was about lust now, not love. A lust that would burn brightly for a while and then gradually fade away just like every other relationship he'd had.

Except with her.

Cristiano sidestepped the thought. He would not allow himself to think like that. This was for now, not for ever. He wasn't a 'for ever' guy now.

He was a 'for the moment' man.

Alice opened her eyes and blinked up at him like a baby owl. 'Is it time to get up?'

Cristiano was already 'up'. His body had been up ten minutes ago when her legs had wrapped around his and her hand had slipped to his abdomen. 'Not yet.' He brushed back her tousled hair. 'There's no hurry.'

She gave him a naughty-girl smile when her hand slid lower and found him fully erect. 'No hurry, huh?'

Cristiano sucked in a breath when her hand started working its wicked magic. She licked her lips and slithered down his body, breathing her sweet hot breath over his abdomen and groin. No one but Alice could reduce him to this—to a quaking wreck of a man without the strength of will to stop her. He barely had time to source a condom before she took him to the stratosphere.

He sank back against the pillows to regain his breath, his arm drawing her close to his side. 'Give me a couple of minutes and I'll be right with you.'

He felt her smile against his chest where her cheek was resting. Her fingers did a piano-playing exercise on his right pectoral muscle. 'Is sex this good with your other partners?' she asked after a moment.

Cristiano had already revealed a little too much in that department. No point giving her more ammunition. 'Fishing, *cara*?'

She made a pouting gesture and went to move away but he held her still. He turned so she was trapped beneath him. She refused to meet his gaze so he inched up her chin so she had no choice. Her blue eyes glittered with resentment but behind that he could see doubt and insecurity moving like shadows. 'I'm not a kiss-and-tell man,' he said. 'I consider it disrespectful.'

Her lashes came down to half-mast over her eyes. After a long moment she released a serrated-sounding breath. 'The last time I had sex I came home and showered for an hour.'

Cristiano's gut clenched as if a steel-studded fist had grabbed his intestines. 'You weren't…?' He couldn't even say the ugly word.

Her lips twisted in a rueful motion. 'No, it was completely consensual, it's just I hated every minute of it. Not that there were too many minutes of it, mind you. Three or four at the most.'

Cristiano brushed back some strands of her tousled hair from her forehead. He hated the thought of her making love with someone else. Hated, hated, *hated* it. For years he'd refused to think about it. He wouldn't allow his mind to torture him with the thought of another man touching her body the way he had touched her, holding her the way he held her. He knew it was arrogant, but he wanted to believe he was the only one who brought that passionate response out of her. *His* body. *His* touch. His need of her triggered the fire in her blood in the same way she triggered his.

'If the chemistry isn't there then the sex will always suffer.'

Her fingertip traced a slow line around his mouth. 'That's something we were never short of, isn't it?' Her words had a faint wistfulness about them.

He captured her finger and kissed the end of it. 'No, that's one thing we had in spades.' In spades and buckets and truck and trailer loads. Still had. He could feel it thrumming between them, the way their bodies meshed as if unable to keep their distance.

Alice linked her arms around his head, her fingers lifting and tugging and releasing the strands of his hair in a way that made every inch of his scalp tingle. 'I've never enjoyed sex with anyone else like I do with you.' Her lips gave a little sideways quirk. 'I should hate you for that. You've ruined my sex life.'

Cristiano gave her a look of mock reproach. 'You haven't done mine any favours, either, young lady.'

Her eyes studied his for a long moment. 'Are you saying it's…better with me?'

He pressed a soft kiss on her forehead. 'It's different.'

Two fine pleats appeared between her eyes. 'How?'

He smoothed away her frown with the pad of his index finger. 'We should get a move on. It will take an hour or so to get to Stresa.'

Her frown snapped back. 'Don't change the subject. Talk to me, Cristiano. Tell me what was different—'

'Look, it just was, okay?' Cristiano rolled away and swung his legs over the edge of the bed. What did she want him to say? That he'd missed her every goddam day since? That every time in the last seven years when he'd touched another woman he'd thought of her? And how much he wished it *were* her? That sex was just sex with anyone else but with her it was making love?

No way was he going to say that.

Even if it was regrettably true.

He heard her sit up on the bed, and then felt her silky hand travel the length of his rigid spine, from his neck to his tailbone, in a soothing caress that made every knob of his vertebrae quiver. She leant her head against his back, her arms going around his waist, the little rush of air from her sigh tickling the skin behind his shoulder blades like the wings of a moth.

'Don't be mad at me,' she said.

Cristiano let out his own sigh and swivelled round to gather her against his side. He dropped a kiss to the top of her head. 'I'm not mad at you, *tesoro*.'

I'm mad at myself.

For still wanting her when he should have been well and truly over her. He wasn't some creepy stalker guy who couldn't let go. There should be no reason he was stuck on her to the point where he couldn't bear to contemplate a future with anyone else. He could have anyone he wanted. He didn't have to fight for dates. If anything, he had to fight them off. But something about

Alice had stayed with him. Like a tune he couldn't get out of his head.

Alice snaked a hand up around his neck, gazing into his eyes with such intensity he wondered if she could sense how much he had missed her. That in spite of all his denials and dissembling she knew—her body knew—he only felt this body-stunning magic with her. Her eyes went to his mouth, her tongue sneaking out to moisten the soft swell of her lips.

'I don't want us to bicker and fight any more. A relationship shouldn't be a competition. It's so...so exhausting.'

Cristiano slid a hand under the curtain of her hair, his mouth coming down to within reach of hers. 'Then we'd better put that energy to much better use, *si*?'

Her eyes shone with anticipation and she lifted her face for his kiss. 'Now you're talking.'

After a quick breakfast, Cristiano drove Alice the ninety-kilometre distance to his grandmother's villa in Stresa situated on the shores of Lake Maggiore. Alice hadn't forgotten how beautiful the lake was with the historic Isola Bella and Isola Superiore a short boat trip from the shore. But seeing it again on a gorgeous autumn morning with the leaves just starting to turn was nothing less than breathtaking.

Cristiano pulled into the driveway of the villa, which had remained empty since his grandmother's death. He'd explained on the journey there that Volante had insisted on dying at home even though he had offered to have her with him in Milan. He had visited as often as he could and Alice was not surprised to hear he had been with Volante when she'd drawn her last breath. But it made her wonder if coming back now his grandmother was gone was far more painful than he was letting on.

Cristiano opened the front door and led the way inside the quiet villa. It was built on a grand scale with dozens of rooms both formal and informal. It was so big it should not have felt like a family home and yet seven years ago it had.

Not now, however.

Now it was a place of ghosts. The furniture was draped in dustsheets and the long corridors and high windows with their curtains drawn were like eyelids closed over tired eyes. Silence crept from every corner. Achingly lonely silence.

Alice slid her hand into Cristiano's, her own eyes suddenly tearing up. 'It must be so hard to come here now. Have you been back since…?'

He squeezed her fingers and turned to look at her. 'No.' His brows came together and he blotted one of her tears with the pad of his thumb. 'She would not want you to cry, *cara*.'

Alice blinked a couple of times and forced a smile to her lips. Their newfound truce was doing strange things to her emotions. Emotions she normally had under the strictest control.

'Sorry. I'm not normally so emotional. I hardly knew her…except I can't help thinking how different this place is without her.' She swiped at her face with the back of her hand. 'I wish I'd written to her. How hard would it have been to send a Christmas card? I just wish I'd let her know I'd never forgotten her, you know?'

He tucked her hand in under his arm. 'You're here now, which is what she wanted.'

Alice still couldn't understand why Volante had left

her a joint share in this villa and with such strange conditions attached. Not only was the villa—even a half-share—worth millions, it was where Cristiano had spent his childhood and adolescence after his family were killed. Surely if anyone deserved the villa it was him? But he had given no indication of being upset about not inheriting it fully. His focus had always been on the shares he stood to lose control of if he didn't fulfil the terms of the will. Even if it meant marrying the woman who had rejected him seven years ago.

'If you'd inherited the villa completely what would you have done with it?' she asked.

He gave a one-shoulder shrug. 'Made it into a hotel.'

'Really? You wouldn't have wanted it as a private retreat?'

He gave her a wry look. 'It's a bit big for one person.'

'Yes, but you might not always be on your own,' Alice said, torturing herself with the thought of who he might spend the rest of his life with. 'You might want to have a family one day. You can become a father at any age so—'

'It's a good location for a hotel,' he said as if she hadn't spoken. 'The gardens too are perfect for weddings and other functions.'

Alice kept her gaze trained on his. 'But doesn't this place mean more to you than that? Don't you have memories you—?'

'What is a house without the people you love inside it?' he said, with a flash of irritation in his gaze. 'It's nothing, that's what it is. It's just bricks and mortar. An empty shell where every room reminds you of someone you've loved and lost.'

Alice swallowed, watching in silence as he tore off

a couple of dustsheets and dropped them to the floor in puddles of white like collapsed sails. She pictured him as a young boy going back to his family's villa after the accident, her heart cramping at the thought of what it had been like for him to walk into that sad vacuum of a place that had once been full of love and laughter.

'I'm so sorry...' Her voice came out little more than a cracked whisper of sound.

He raked a hand through his hair and let out a long rough sigh. 'No, I'm the one who's sorry. I shouldn't have spoken so harshly to you. Forgive me.'

Alice closed the distance between them and slipped her arms around his waist, looking up at his grimly set features. 'It's fine. This is really painful for you.'

After a moment his expression softened a fraction as if her presence calmed him. He gave her a twist of a smile, his hand brushing an imaginary hair away from her face.

'I should have been back here weeks ago. I just couldn't seem to do it. I didn't want to face this place without her in it. It reminded me too much of the trip home after my parents and brother were killed.'

Alice moved her arms from around his waist and took his hands in hers, gently stroking their strong backs with her thumbs. 'I can't imagine how that must have been for you.'

He looked down at their joined hands for a moment before returning his gaze to hers. 'My grandparents tried to spare me the trauma of going back home but I insisted. It was weird...surreal, really. Everything at home looked the same but it was different. It was like the villa was holding its breath or something.'

His gaze got a faraway look and shifted from hers.

'It was like my life had been jammed on pause. I stood there thinking if only I could turn back the clock. Maybe if I hadn't been sick they wouldn't have had to make the detour to my grandparents' place, then they wouldn't have been on that road at that particular time.'

Alice clutched at his hands. 'You mustn't blame yourself. You were a child. Kids get sick all the time. You can't possibly blame yourself for someone else's stupidity. It was that drunk driver's fault, not yours, that your family were killed.'

Cristiano's fingers shifted against hers, his eyes still shadowed.

'I was cautious about expressing my grief because it only made it harder on my grandparents. If I showed how devastated I was then they would have that to deal with along with everything else. They were so strong but it can't have been easy bringing up a child at their stage of life. They'd stepped back from the hotel business to enjoy a quieter life, but of course all that changed. My grandfather had to run things until I was of an age to take over.'

He slipped his hands out of hers and walked over to one of the windows that overlooked the lake.

Alice wanted to follow him but sensed he was gathering himself. She couldn't recall a time when he had spoken with such depth about his loss. He had never seemed to want to talk about it before. Why hadn't she taken the time to encourage him to unburden himself? She had been so immature back then she hadn't seen how the loss of his family was why he over-controlled everything. She had been mulish and opinionated instead of compassionate and understanding. If only she had been less focussed on her own opinions she might have realised how tragic his life had been and how it had coloured everything he did.

Her background had its issues, certainly, but nothing compared to what he'd been through. She looked at his tall frame standing there and pictured the child he had once been. Trying to be strong for his grandparents. Containing his grief to protect them. Hadn't she done the same with her mother? Tried to be strong, becoming the adult instead of the child in order to help her mother through every broken relationship. Ignoring her own needs until she could barely recognise them when they cropped up. 'Oh, Cristiano...'

He turned and looked at her with one of his smiles that wasn't quite a smile. 'You know what's ironic? My brother was the one with his heart set on taking over the business. I had other plans.'

Shock ran through Alice in an icy tide. Plans? What plans? How had she spent six weeks with this man and not once realised he'd had other plans for his life than the hotel business? He was so successful. He owned and operated some of the most luxurious boutique hotels in the Mediterranean. When you thought of boutique hotels you thought of Cristiano Marchetti. But what had *he* wanted to do with his life?

'You mean you didn't want to be in the hotel business? Not at all?'

He picked up a photograph of his grandparents as a young couple that was on the walnut table near the window, his fingers moving over the carved frame as if he were reading Braille.

'No. I wanted to be an architect. But it was impossible once my parents and brother died. I don't think I even mentioned it to my grandparents after that. I knew my fate. The responsibility was ultimately mine otherwise everything my parents and grandparents had worked for would be lost. I had to shelve my plans and immerse myself in the business. But don't feel too sorry for me, *cara*.'

He put the photograph back down and glanced at her.

'I have plenty of opportunity to express my creativity when I'm working on renovating an old building.' His mouth twisted in a self-deprecating manner. 'I make the architect's life hell for a few months but that's life.'

Alice was in a turmoil of regret over not realising any of this until now. She had made so many assumptions about him. She had even playfully mocked him about his wealth on occasion. And not so playfully recently, when she'd made that crack about all the silver spoons hanging out of his mouth.

All the clues were there now she stopped to reflect on their time together. He had been reluctant to talk about his past because he found it so painful. Not just because of the loss of his family but the loss of the life he had mapped out for himself. He had lost control of everything the day his parents and brother were killed.

She thought of all the times she had talked to him about her plans to build her own beauty spa. She had told him how she had wanted to do it since she was a little girl when she went with her mother to a beauty salon when her mother got her nails done for her second wedding. Alice had been captivated by all the lotions and potions and the sense of luxury so unfamiliar in her life back then. She'd made a decision right then and there to own and operate her own beauty salon where women could escape the humdrum of life and spoil themselves with some pampering. She had fought for her dream and achieved it in spite of the disadvantages of her background.

But Cristiano's background—the one she had envied so much—had been the cause of him *not* being able to live his dream.

Alice walked over to where he was standing and placed her hand on his forearm. 'I've always felt jealous of your wealth, that you could buy anything you want, travel anywhere you like, do anything you like. But it's been more of a burden than anything else, hasn't it?'

He placed his hand over hers, bringing it up to his chest. 'It's both a blessing and a burden but I would much rather have the security of wealth than not. Don't get me wrong. I enjoy my work. I didn't for a long time, but I do now.'

'But who will take over from you once you get to retirement age?' Alice asked. 'Your cousin?'

'God no,' he said with a roll of his eyes. 'Rocco has no head for business. His idea of a hotel makeover would be to install slot machines in every room. My parents and grandparents would spin in their graves.' He sighed and released her hand. 'No, I'll probably sell the business outright when the time is right.'

'But if you had a family, a son or daughter, they could take over and—'

'You seem a little hung up on this issue, Alice.' His tone was on the edge of being crisp. 'Does this mean you've changed your mind about having children?'

Alice forced herself to hold his gaze. 'We're not talking about me. We're talking about you. You have so much to offer a child. You have a strong sense of family. You've had great modelling in both your parents and grandparents. Why wouldn't you pass on that wonderful heritage to your own offspring?'

'Let's talk about you, then,' he said, his gaze unwavering. 'Who will you leave your goods and chattels to? A dog's home?'

Alice pursed her lips and then puffed out a sigh. If they were supposed to be working at a truce then why shouldn't she be honest with him?

She shook back her hair and raised her gaze back to his. 'Okay, I'll let you in on a secret. I have thought about having kids. I've thought about it a lot recently.'

'And?'

'And it's something I'd like to do one day. When I find the right man, of course.'

His expression became shuttered. 'What made you change your mind?'

Alice picked up another photo next to the one of his grandparents. It was a family shot of Cristiano with his parents and older brother. She had seen it before without really seeing it. Cristiano was a happy child in that photo, smiling with an open and engaging expression. Nothing like the serious and closed-off man of today. She put the photo back down and looked at him again.

'It was a gradual thing rather than an overnight change of heart,' she said.

Not unlike my feelings for you.

'I realised what I'd be missing out on when I saw my friends and my clients with their babies. It's such a special relationship—unique, really—the love between a mother and child.' She gave him a flutter of a smile. 'My mother drives me completely nuts but deep down I know she loves me more than anyone else on this planet. I want to feel that love. I want to experience that bond.'

His mouth turned up at one side in a rueful angle. 'What a pity my grandmother meddled with your life. You'll have to put your baby plans on hold for another six months.'

Alice shifted her gaze. 'Yes, well, I'm only twenty-eight. I don't have to panic just yet.'

There was an odd little silence.

Alice wondered if he was thinking of the irony of their situation. He had desperately wanted a family seven years ago while she had wanted her freedom. Now he wanted his freedom while she was peering into every pram that went past.

What if she didn't find a man she could love enough to father her children? But who else could she want but Cristiano? Her feelings for him had been on slow burn in her heart. Banked down out of bitterness because he hadn't fought for her in the past. But the more she thought about her future, she couldn't imagine sharing it with anyone other than him. She would rather be alone than be with someone else.

Maybe that was why she had panicked and pushed him away. She had seen him as the one man who could make her sacrifice the dream of owning her own business. It had been too confronting for her as a twenty-one-year-old on the threshold of her life. Too threatening in case he hadn't loved her enough to give her the freedom to pursue her own goals instead of subsuming her life into the powerful engine of his.

But now...now she had established her business. She knew who she was and what she wanted for her life. And that included the things he no longer wanted. Marriage. A family. To love and be loved.

But Cristiano no longer loved her, if he ever had.

The only reason he was with her now was because of the shares that hung in the balance. If it hadn't been for his grandmother's will she would never have heard from him again. She had to remember that. He was only marrying her to get what he wanted. He might still desire her but he was a full-blooded man with a healthy appetite for sex.

This thing they had going on was for now, not for ever.

CHAPTER NINE

CRISTIANO LED ALICE through the villa but his mind was preoccupied.

She wanted a family.

After all those heated arguments in the past over not wanting kids. It had been a sticking point in their relationship. He had thought her selfish for putting her career above having a family. Selfish and unnatural. But now he was the one who was career focussed. He had made himself so busy he couldn't find time for a steady relationship, let alone a family that would need nurturing day by day, week by week, year by year. He didn't want it because the thought of losing it was too terrifying. Too awful to even contemplate.

He knew all too well how it felt to have his world ripped out from under him. Once was enough. More than enough. Loving someone meant you could lose them. You could lose part of yourself and never get it back.

'May I see the garden now?' Alice said, breaking through his reverie.

'Sure.' Cristiano took her hand and led her to the French doors leading out to the terrace. 'This was one of my grandmother's favourite places. She would sit out here for hours watching the birdlife in the garden.'

'It's such a beautiful place.' Alice's voice had a reverent note to it. 'Around every corner is another surprise. It's like a story unfolding.'

Cristiano waited on the terrace while she wandered about the garden. She stopped to smell the roses his grandmother had planted as a young bride, her fingers softly touching the fragrant petals. The sun caught her hair and turned it into a skein of shining silver, and she brushed some strands away from her face that the light breeze had toyed with and tucked them back behind her ear. She caught him looking at her and gave him a smile that made something inside his chest ache.

'This would make a great wedding venue, don't you think?' she said. 'The wisteria walk would be a gorgeous place for the bride to walk towards the groom.'

'Would you like to get married here?' Cristiano asked.

A slight frown creased her smooth brow. 'But I thought you wanted a church wedding?'

He shrugged. 'As long as it's legal who cares where it's conducted?'

She pulled at her lower lip with her teeth and turned slightly to look at the angel fountain his grandmother had installed after the stillborn birth of her first child the year before Cristiano's father had been born. So much of his family's history was embedded in this place. There wasn't a shrub or tree or yew hedge that hadn't witnessed a Marchetti triumph or tragedy.

After a moment Alice turned to look at him. 'To be honest, I'd rather be married here than in a church. It would make it less...' She seemed to be searching for the right word and bit into her lip again.

'Binding?' Cristiano said.

Her mouth went into a flat line. 'Don't you feel the slightest bit uncomfortable about all this? Marriage is a big deal. As the words of the ceremony say: it's not to be entered into lightly.'

Was she having second thoughts? His guts churned. If she didn't marry him he would lose the shares and the villa. He couldn't allow that to happen.

'Look at it this way. We're fulfilling an old lady's dying wishes by getting married. It's not about us. It's about Nonna. And I think she would be thrilled if we had the ceremony here. I'll get working on it straight away.' He held his hand out for hers, drawing her against his side. 'Now, let's make the most of the day here in Stresa.'

It was a lovely day in spite of Alice's misgivings about where things were heading in their relationship. Cristiano organised a private tour of the islands and a gorgeous lunch at a restaurant by the lake. They drove back to Milan late in the afternoon and, after a quick shower and freshen up, he took her to one of the city's premier restaurants, where the maître d' welcomed Cristiano by name and showered them with effusive congratulations and a bottle of champagne on the house.

Alice sat opposite him sipping her champagne and wondered if he was thinking about that other restaurant only a few streets from here where he had proposed to her while the rest of the diners looked on. With the benefit of hindsight, she wished she'd handled it a little better than she had. But the shock of his sudden proposal after only a few weeks of dating had thrown her into a panic.

Surely she could have let him down without publicly humiliating him. Why had she been so crass and immature? How must he have felt to be left in that restaurant with everyone staring at him open-mouthed? The ring he'd chosen thrown onto the table as if it were a cheap fairground trinket. She hadn't even gone back to his villa, because her passport had been in her tote bag, and she'd caught a taxi straight to the airport and got on the first flight she could.

'More champagne?' Cristiano asked into the silence.

Alice put her hand over the top of her glass. 'Better not. I've had too much already.'

'You're not driving so if you want another I don't mind.'

She waited a couple of beats. 'Did you ever meet the person who—?'

'No.' The word was delivered with such finality it sounded like a gavel falling.

Alice moistened her lips. 'Did they express any remorse? Make any effort to contact you or your grandparents?'

His mouth was twisted in an embittered line. 'No. He was the sort of person who blamed everyone but himself for his wrongdoing. He didn't even get jail time. The judge overseeing the case had connections with his influential father. But karma got him in the end. He was killed in a bar fight. A drug deal gone sour.' He shifted his water glass half a centimetre and then did a slow tap of his fingers on the tablecloth. 'I thought it would help to know he'd got his comeuppance, but strangely it didn't.'

Alice reached across the table and grasped his hand. 'That's because you're not at heart a vengeful man.'

His half-smile was a little crooked. 'Am I not?' His fingers toyed with her engagement ring. 'You would not have liked what I was thinking when you stormed out of that restaurant seven years ago.'

She looked at their joined hands rather than meet his gaze. 'I'm sorry I reacted the way I did back then. It was so...so petulant and immature of me to behave like that.'

He gave her hand a quick squeeze before he released it to sit back in his chair. 'I shouldn't have put you under so much pressure. I was in too much of a rush after my grandfather died.' He did that slow tapping thing again next to his glass, his forehead creasing in a frown. 'Funerals can do that to you. Make you realise how fragile life is.'

Alice thought about him attending his family's funerals, the weight of grief he'd had to shoulder so bravely as a child, and then as an adult saying goodbye to each of his grandparents in turn. She had only been to one funeral—an elderly client who had passed away after a short illness. It had been sad but not tragic. Her family had celebrated her long life and sent her off with a party that had gone on until the early hours of the morning. What did Alice know of how it must feel to say that final goodbye to someone so beloved as a parent, grandparent or sibling?

'All the same, I wish I'd been a little kinder to you.' She let out a tiny sigh. 'I guess that's why you didn't contact me.'

Something flickered in his gaze. Surprise? Alarm? Regret? It was hard to distinguish which. 'Did you want me to?'

Alice wasn't sure it served any purpose to admit to how much she'd hoped he would. What was done was done. It was in the past and best left there. 'No. We were over as far as I was concerned.'

His eyes held hers for a long beat or two. 'How soon did you date someone else?'

She gave a little shrug. 'I don't know...six or so months maybe.' She flashed him a brittle glance before she could stop herself. 'Certainly longer than it took you.'

There was a small silence.

'I made sure I was seen with other women within days of us breaking up,' he said. 'But it was eight months before I could bring myself to sleep with anyone.'

Alice flickered her eyelids in shock. He'd waited *that* long? 'Eight months? Really?'

He gave a grim nod. 'It just didn't feel right rushing into another intense relationship.'

'It was pretty intense, wasn't it?'

He gave that sexy half-smile again and reached for her hand. 'It still is.'

The door was barely closed behind them when they returned to Cristiano's villa when he reached for her. The drive home from the restaurant had been a form of foreplay. His looks, his touch on her thigh when he changed the gears, the throb and roar of the engine that reminded Alice of the potent hormones surging through his body. His mouth came down on hers in a scorching kiss, his tongue tangling with hers in a provocative duel that made her tingle with anticipation.

She tore at his clothes with desperate hands, sliding her palms over the warm hard flesh of his chest and abdomen. He shrugged off his shirt and set to work on her dress, ripping down the zipper at the back and sliding his hand down the length of her spine, holding her against his pulsing heat. He brought his mouth to her neck and décolletage, his lips and tongue lighting spot fires beneath her skin. His hands cupped her breasts from below, pushing them upwards for the descent of his mouth.

She gasped out her pleasure when his mouth closed over one tightly budded nipple, his tongue swirling around the sensitive areola until she was sagging at the knees.

Alice sent her hands lower to free him from his trousers and underwear, taking him in her hand and stroking and squeezing him the way she knew he liked. He groaned his approval against her breast, creating a buzzing sensation that made the hairs on her scalp lift in a Mexican wave.

He lifted his mouth from her breast, his voice low and deep and gravelly with desire. *'Ti desidero.'*

'I want you too.'

He lifted her in one effortless swoop and carried her upstairs to his bedroom. He laid her on the mattress and, after dispensing with the rest of his clothes, dealt with the rest of hers. But somewhere along the way he slowed down the mad pace of his lovemaking and subjected her to an exquisite worship of her body from head to foot that made every cell throb and vibrate with need. His lips, his tongue, his hands, even his breath skating over her skin built her desire to fever pitch until she was all but begging for mercy.

'How much do you want me?' he said against her belly, his stubble grazing her skin.

'So much. Oh, please...*please*...' She writhed and twisted, aching for that final push.

He sheathed himself with a condom and entered her in a thick thrust that set off an explosion in her swollen flesh. She arched her spine to keep the contact where she needed it, the rioting sensations shooting through her like fireworks. She had barely recovered from that first orgasm when another one followed, a deeper one that rolled through her in tumultuous waves.

The contractions of her body must have triggered his own for he tensed all over and then surged deeper into her and shuddered and spilled.

Alice flung her head back against the pillows with a blissful sigh. 'Wow. Double wow.'

He propped himself up on his elbows and traced a fingertip down between her breasts. 'Not many women can orgasm like that without direct stimulation.'

She smiled and stroked a hand down his muscled arm. 'So I'm special, am I?'

His gaze intensified. 'You're the most responsive lover I've ever had.'

Alice tiptoed her fingers over his bicep. 'That's really saying something since you've had so many and all.'

He frowned at her tone and moved away to deal with the condom. 'You shouldn't believe everything you read in the press. If I'd bedded even half the women the press said I had, I wouldn't have had time to run my business.'

Alice sat up and reached for the throw on the end of the bed, wrapping it around her body. She was annoyed for broadcasting her jealousy again. How would she be able to walk away from their relationship with any dignity once it was time to go if she kept yammering on about his playboy lifestyle? He had a perfect right to have lovers. Numerous lovers.

No one had stopped her doing the same. No one but her, that was. She should be feeling happy he had at least refrained from bringing anyone back to his villa since her. That was huge. And the fact he had waited eight months surely should make her feel a little mollified, but sadly it didn't. He might not have moved on as quickly as the press had reported but neither had he come after her. He had kept his distance and seven long years had gone past. Seven years they could have had together...

She stood from the bed. 'I'm going to take off my make-up.'

He came to stand in front of her, his expression softening. 'I thought we agreed not to take cheap shots at each other.'

Alice rolled her lips together and then sighed. 'I'm sorry.'

He lifted her chin, brushing his thumb over her lower lip. 'I want us to be friends when this is over. It's what my grandmother would've wanted.'

'You don't think she wanted us to...to make a go of it?'

His hand fell away from her face. 'If she did then that's too bad because it's not going to happen.'

But it could if he wanted it to.

Alice tried to ignore the tight spasm of her heart. He was ruling out any possibility of them being a proper couple. Refusing to contemplate a future with her. A future with all the things she longed for now. What a cruel quirk of fate to have their roles reversed.

'Did I say I wanted it to? I'm just saying she probably had it in mind when she conjured up this scheme. At the very least she would've wanted us to settle our differences.'

Cristiano ran a hand through his hair. 'We've done that.'

'Have we?'

He let out a long breath and stepped close to her again, cupping her cheek in one broad hand, his dark chocolate eyes holding hers. 'You no longer hate me, do you, *cara*?'

I never hated you.

Alice gave him a wobbly smile. 'Do you still hate me?'

He brought his mouth down to within a millimetre of hers. 'Does this feel like hate to you?' And covered her mouth with his.

It felt like heaven.

When Alice got back to work on Monday it was like stepping into controlled chaos.

Meghan greeted her with a beaming smile from behind the reception counter. 'You would not believe the number of clients who want to see you. You're fully booked for months and months. Years probably. Your engagement to Cristiano Marchetti has opened doors. Big doors. Guess which Hollywood superstar wants you to do their make-up for their wedding in November? You'll never ever guess.'

She pulled out a chair and pushed it towards Alice.

'Here, you'd better sit down before I tell you.'

Alice ignored the chair. 'It's all right—I won't faint. Who is it?'

Meghan named a rising-star female actor who was the current toast of Hollywood.

'And that's not all,' she continued in a rush of excitement. 'She's going to fly you, all expenses paid, to the wedding location. It's top secret so as to keep the press away so you won't be told until the very last moment. You'll have to sign a confidentiality agreement.

I bet it's going to be in Bora Bora or maybe at Richard Branson's place, you know, Necker Island. Or maybe St Bart's. Oh, God, imagine if it was in St Bart's. You'll need an assistant, won't you?' She clasped her hands as if in prayer. 'Take me with you? Please, please, please?'

Alice laughed at the exuberant puppy-like look on her young employee's face. 'I'll have to see if the booking comes off first. No point getting too excited. You know what some of those Hollywood celebrities are like. Their weddings are cancelled at a moment's notice.'

Some of Meghan's enthusiasm sagged. 'True, but if it goes ahead things will never be the same around here. You'll be the wedding make-up artist to the stars.'

I have to get through my own 'wedding' first.

Alice's first client of the day a few days later was a bride-to-be who was booked in for a trial make-up session.

Jennifer Preston was the epitome of a woman radiantly in love. She had been coming to Alice for years as a client and somehow over the time their relationship had morphed into friendship. Jennifer had always bemoaned the fact she hadn't been able to find a suitable partner. But now she was happily engaged to a man she had met on a blind date set up by a friend and it truly was a match made in heaven.

Even a hardened cynic like Alice had to admit love at first sight could happen. Jennifer's fiancé, Marcus, dropped her off at her appointment, and the way he looked at Jennifer when he kissed her goodbye made Alice feel like an imposter. Not that Cristiano didn't look at her with affection and tenderness, but it wasn't as if he were truly in love with her as Marcus was with Jennifer and had been from the moment they'd met.

During Jennifer's trial make-up session, she told Alice about her wedding dress and the romantic honeymoon Marcus had planned. 'You know, Alice, a few months ago I was single and hating it,' Jennifer said. 'Now I'm getting married to a man I adore and he adores me. But you know what I'm talking about. That man of yours is a seriously fast worker. Have you chosen your dress?'

'Erm… Not yet, but I plan to duck out between clients this afternoon,' Alice said. 'So much to do, so little time.'

Jennifer rolled her eyes. 'Tell me about it.' She leaned forward to check her make-up. 'Gosh, you've done a brilliant job. I look almost beautiful.'

Alice put her hand on Jennifer's shoulder and gave it a squeeze. 'You *are* beautiful. You're positively glowing.'

Jennifer placed her hand over Alice's, her eyes shimmering with excitement. 'I haven't told anyone else but Marcus yet, but I'm pregnant. Six weeks. Will you be godmother when it's born?'

Alice blinked in surprise. 'Me?'

Jennifer swung the chair around so she was facing Alice instead of talking to her reflection in the mirror. She grasped Alice's hands in hers. 'Why not you? You and I have been banging on about the paucity of good men in London for the last seven years. Now we're both getting married within weeks of each other. And who knows? Maybe you'll get pregnant soon too.'

Alice stretched her mouth into a smile that felt as fake as her upcoming wedding. 'I'd be thrilled to be godmother. Truly honoured.'

Jennifer smiled. 'That's settled, then. Of course, you're bringing Cristiano to my wedding? I'll talk to the wedding planner about changing the seating arrangements. I've put you on a great table.'

'That's very kind,' Alice said. 'I'll have to check with him to see if he's free that weekend.'

'I'm sure he'd do anything for you,' Jennifer said, eyes sparkling. 'He's a man in love, right?'

CHAPTER TEN

ALICE RUSHED OUT between clients to check a couple of wedding boutiques in the area but couldn't see anything that captured her attention. Or maybe it was her mood that was the problem. She'd been fighting a tension headache all afternoon. It didn't feel right trying on dresses for a wedding that wasn't going to last. It wasn't just the expense of a dress, which was astronomical at the top end of town, but more the thought of play-acting at bride and groom when all she wanted was for it to be real.

How different would this shopping trip be if she were a bride like Jennifer Preston? Trying on beautiful gowns and veils, imagining Cristiano's face at the end of the aisle when she appeared at the church.

Maybe even carrying his baby...

Instead, Alice was going through the motions of bridal preparation knowing in her heart that her relationship with Cristiano was doomed for despair. If he'd wanted their relationship to be for ever then surely he would have said something by now?

She had spent every night with him since they'd come back from Italy. Their relationship had settled into a less combative one but was no less exciting. Every time he looked at her, she felt the rush of attraction course through her flesh. The dark glint in his eyes was enough to make her shudder with excitement.

Like this morning, for instance. He had given her that look and she had put aside her breakfast and made mad passionate love with him up against the kitchen bench. His touch was as magical as ever, in some ways even more intensely satisfying than in the past. Or maybe that was because Alice knew his touching of her was only temporary, that within a few months they would part and go their separate ways. The thought of it was heart-wrenching. How had it taken her this long to re-alise she loved him?

Or had she always loved him?

Was that why his proposal had been so threatening? She hadn't been ready to admit to how she felt about him. She'd needed more time. More time to question the opinions she'd formed out of fear, not facts. Loving someone back then had felt like giving up a part of herself and never getting it back. But true love shouldn't be like that, surely?

True love was supposed to build up, not destroy.

To heal and create harmony, not hurt and dissension.

'Can I help you with anything?' a shop assistant asked in the last bridal boutique Alice wandered into. 'Oh, my goodness! You're Alice Piper, the wedding make-up celebrity. You did my friend's wedding make-up last year. Congratulations, by the way. Gosh, what an honour, you coming in here for your wedding dress. Let me show you around. Did you have a budget in mind?'

'Erm… I'm just looking at the moment,' Alice said, wondering how she could back out of the shop before the woman gave the paparazzi a heads up to boost her business. She wasn't the best shopper under pressure as it was. She needed time to think. Time to reflect. The last thing she needed right now was the press showing up and flashing cameras and microphones in her face.

The woman frowned. 'But aren't you getting married, like, in a couple of weeks?'

Don't remind me how close it is!

'October first,' Alice said, trying to ignore her thumping heartbeat and the beads of perspiration breaking out on her upper lip.

Cristiano had confirmed the details a few days ago. Their flights were booked, the staff notified at his grandmother's villa to get the place ready for a small wedding party. It was all happening so quickly and yet she felt on the perimeter of it all, like an observer on the sidelines.

'We can still get something made in time.' The woman gave Alice an obsequious smile. 'Especially for someone of *your* status. Nothing off the rack for Cristiano Marchetti's bride, hey? How about we look at some designs?' She whipped out a bridal magazine and fanned the pages open. 'White? Cream? Lace? Satin? Organza?'

Alice swallowed a ropey knot of panic. So many dresses… Who knew there were so many shades of white and cream? So many designs. So many decisions to make. So little time. How did brides do this without having a meltdown? No wonder so many of them got the Bridezilla tag.

The boutique was suddenly too hot, too stuffy, as if someone had sucked all the oxygen out of the room. Her head was in a vice, the pressure mounting until it felt as if her brain were going to explode through her skull.

She swayed on her feet, her vision blurring. The walls were buckling, closing in on her. Nausea churned in her stomach and then climbed up her throat on sticky claws.

'Are you all right?' The shop assistant grasped Alice by the arm. 'Here, sit down and put your head between your knees.'

Alice sank to the velvet-covered chair and lowered her head to her lap. She was vaguely aware of the shop assistant talking to someone on the phone and then a glass of water being handed to her. She sat up to take a few sips but the room was still spinning.

The woman took the glass from her. 'I've called an ambulance. They should be here soon.'

Alice looked up at her in alarm, her heart hammering like a drummer on crack. 'I don't need an ambulance.'

There was the sound of a siren screaming outside. It echoed the silent scream inside Alice's head. *No-o-o-o-o!*

'Too late,' the woman said. 'Here, give me your phone. I'll call your fiancé for you.'

Alice clutched her bag against her body as if it contained the Crown Jewels. 'It's all right—I'll call him. I don't want him to panic over nothing.'

The woman tottered away to greet the paramedics coming through the door. 'She's over there. She nearly fainted. She was talking to me as good as anything and then she went as white as that dress in the window. I reckon she's pregnant. I was exactly the same when I had my daughters.'

Shoot me now.

Cristiano had finished with his meeting with the architectural firm he'd employed to do the designs for the makeover of his Chelsea building so decided to call in at Alice's salon to see if she was finished for the day. He could have called or texted her, but he knew she kept her phone on silent when at work and sometimes forgot to unmute it. Besides, he liked seeing her in her work environment. She was always so professional but he got a kick out of knowing that behind that cool and composed façade and that neat little uniform was a feisty and passionate woman who came apart in his arms.

But when he walked into the salon Meghan, her assistant, was in a flustered state.

'Why are you here?' she said. 'Shouldn't you be at the hospital?'

Cristiano's stomach dropped like an anvil hitting concrete. 'Hospital?'

Meghan was wide-eyed with strain. 'Yes, Alice fainted in a shop. I got a call from the owner a few minutes ago. She said Alice has been taken to hospital for observation. I've been in such a state trying to cancel all her clients as well as do my own. Is she all right? What's wrong with her? They wouldn't let me speak to her.'

Cristiano's heart was giving a very good impression of needing urgent medical attention itself.

Alice sick? Taken to hospital?

Panic pounded like thunder in his blood.

No. No. No. Not again.

What if he couldn't get there in time? Things happened in hospitals. Bad things. People went in and didn't always come out. Or they did, but in body bags just like his family. 'Which hospital?'

Meghan told him and then added as he rushed out of the door, 'Oh, my God. You didn't know?'

'My phone's been off all afternoon.' He took it out of his jacket pocket and almost dropped it in his haste. But there were no missed calls from Alice and no text messages, either. What did that mean? She couldn't call because she was too ill? Unconscious? In a coma?

His heart flapped like a blown tyre. His pulse hammered. He was so consumed with dread it felt as if a pineapple were jammed halfway down his throat.

'Tell her I've got everything under control here,' Meghan called after him. 'Well, sort of…'

Cristiano hailed the nearest cab and then spent the entire journey wishing he'd dragged the cabby out of the driver's seat and driven the thing himself. By the time he got to the hospital he was so worked up he could barely speak. He had to draw in a couple of deep breaths when he walked through the door.

The clean antiseptic smell hit him like a slap, instantly transporting him to that dreadful day. After his parents and brother were killed he had gone with his grandparents to the hospital where they had been taken. He still remembered those long corridors with the sound of his trainers squeaking as he walked that agonising walk to where his family were lying lifeless. He remembered the looks from the doctors and nurses—a mixture of compassion, I'm-glad-it's-not-my-loved-ones-lying-in-there, and business-as-usual indifference. He remembered the shock of seeing his mother's and father's and brother's bodies draped in shroud-like sheets. Not being able to grasp the thought of them never coming home, of life never being the same.

It had felt as if he had stepped into a parallel universe—it hadn't been him standing there looking at his family but some other kid. Someone who *could* deal with it. Someone who wouldn't carry the wound of loss around for the rest of his life.

Cristiano found the emergency department and asked a nurse for Alice's whereabouts in a voice that sounded nothing like his own. He was led to a cubicle where Alice was lying with her eyes closed and hooked up to a saline drip. He saw the rise and fall of her chest and a giant wave of relief swept through him. He opened his mouth to say her name but nothing came out. He reached for her hand not attached to the drip and she opened her eyes and gave him a tremulous smile. 'Hi.'

He sank to the chair beside the bed because he was sure his legs were going to fold beneath him.

'What happened? What's wrong, *cara*? Are you unwell? I was so worried I thought you might be…' He swallowed back the word. 'You scared the hell out of me. Are you all right?'

'I'm perfectly fine. I just got a bit dehydrated and almost passed out. I didn't want all this fuss but the lady in the shop I was in was so pushy and—'

'It was a good thing she was,' Cristiano said. 'Why haven't you been drinking enough? Are you not feeling well? You should have said—'

'I was busy, that's all.' She gave him a weary smile. 'Since we got back from Italy I've been run off my feet. I didn't get lunch and I hadn't had anything to drink since breakfast and that was only a sip or two of tea.'

He cradled her hand in both of his. Guilt slammed through him. It was his fault she hadn't had a proper breakfast. He had distracted her with a passionate kiss that had ended with them making love up against the kitchen bench. He couldn't resist her when she was all dressed up for work in that crisp smart uniform. He couldn't resist her, period. He brought her hand up to his mouth and gently pressed a kiss to it.

'How soon before I can take you home or do they want to keep you in overnight?'

She lifted her arm connected to the cannula. 'Just until this runs through.'

Cristiano stroked her fingers. 'You almost gave me a heart attack, young lady.'

She gave him a rueful movement of her lips. 'Sorry.'

'What shop were you in?'

Her gaze fell away from his. 'A bridal boutique.'

Cristiano made a 'that figures' sound. 'Yeah, well, I felt like passing out when I came in here. Bridal boutiques aren't your favourite haunts and hospitals aren't mine.'

Her gaze came back to his, her brow wrinkled in concern. 'I'm so sorry for making you panic. I didn't want anyone to call you. I knew I'd be all right once I got some fluids on board.'

Why hadn't she got someone to call him? Didn't she realise how that made him feel? Didn't she have an inkling of what he'd gone through just then? 'But you should have called me or had someone do it for you.'

Her frown deepened. 'Why should I?'

He gave her a speaking look. 'Come on, Alice, we're engaged to be married, for God's sake. I'm the first person you or someone taking care of you should call when something like this happens.'

Her gaze slipped out of reach of his. 'We're not exactly like a normal couple, though, are we?'

Cristiano tightened his hold on her hand. 'This isn't the time or place to have this conversation. You're not well and I'm in no state to be rational.'

There was a long silence.

'Aren't you going to ask?' Alice said.

'Ask what?'

She turned her head to meet his gaze. 'Whether I'm pregnant.'

Cristiano's heart juddered to a stop and then started again with a sickening jolt. 'Are you?'

'No.'

He was glad...*wasn't he*? Of course he was. A baby was the last thing he wanted. A baby would change everything. He didn't want anything changed. Their marriage was two weeks away and that was all he wanted to think about right now. Get the job done. Mission accomplished. Move on.

'That's good.' He gave her hand a reassuring squeeze. 'I bet you're relieved about that.'

Another weary smile flickered across her mouth. 'Sure am.' She shifted on the bed as if the mattress was uncomfortable. 'I've been asked to be godmother to a client-stroke-friend's baby. I'm going to her wedding after I do her make-up next weekend. She's invited you since we're...you know, supposed to be engaged.'

'Would you like me to go with you?'

Her teeth sank into the pillow of her lip for a moment. 'I guess it'll be a good practice run, huh? See how it's done and all.'

'You've been to a wedding before, surely? Or has your aversion to them stretched that far?'

'I was flower girl at my mother's second marriage,' Alice said. 'I tripped going up the aisle and my stepfather told me off for it afterwards in front of all the guests. I was so mortified I wet my pants.'

Cristiano frowned. 'How old were you?'

'Six. He carried on about it for years and my mother never did anything to stop him.' She gave a little sigh. 'I was glad when he left her for another woman. But for a while after Mum blamed me for jinxing their wedding day.'

'Does she still blame you?'

'No, not now.' Another sigh wafted past her lips. 'But I didn't go to her third wedding on principle.'

'In case you tripped up the aisle?'

She gave him a worldly look. 'No, because her third husband has wandering hands and is a thief.'

Cristiano could see now why she had a thing about marriage. 'What about your father? Did he ever marry again?'

'Yes, and surprisingly it's working,' she said. 'He and Tania haven't had it easy, though. They have a little boy with severe autism. That's why I give Dad money from time to time, to pay for Sam's therapy.'

'That's kind of you.'

She gave a little movement of her lips that could have loosely passed for a smile. 'My dad isn't as bad as my mother always makes out. He just wasn't ready for marriage way back then. He's grown up now. He's taking responsibility for his wife and family. I know he wasn't an angel by any means when he was married to my mother, but he wasn't in love with her. Not the way he is with Tania.'

Her fingers plucked at the hem of the sheet.

'I guess that's what makes or breaks a marriage. Whether the love is strong enough to cope with what life dishes up.'

The nurse came in at that point and Cristiano moved aside so she could detach the drip from Alice's arm. He couldn't help thinking of how little he had known of Alice's background in the past. Why hadn't he asked her more about her childhood? Why hadn't he told her more about his?

They had been two people madly in lust with each other, sharing their bodies but not sharing their hearts and minds. Not communicating other than on a physical level. He had found out more about her in this hospital cubicle than he had in the whole time he had dated her in the past. Would it have made a difference if he'd talked to her? Really talked to her?

'You're good to go,' the nurse said once the drip was out and the paperwork dealt with. 'Take care of yourself, Alice. Keep those fluids up and get plenty of rest, okay?'

'I'll make sure she does,' Cristiano said.

Alice walked out of the hospital with Cristiano's arm around her waist. Her headache had eased and her stomach had stopped its churning. He had looked so undone by her being sick. She had never seen him look so distressed. Did that mean he cared more about her than he let on? Surely it wasn't an act for the sake of appearances?

But then there was a lot hanging in the balance. If she didn't fulfil the terms of the will then he would lose those shares and the home he had grown up in after his family were killed.

Or was that why he had been so rattled? Because hospitals reminded him of the accident that had taken his family from him?

Cristiano hailed a cab and within a short while they were home at her house and she was tucked up in bed with a long cool glass of water with a slice of lemon and ice cubes in it. He sat on the edge of the bed beside her, his hand taking one of hers in a gentle hold. 'How are you feeling?'

'Tired and a bit embarrassed about all the fuss I've caused.'

His fingers stroked the back of her hand. 'Yeah, well, you certainly gave me a bad half an hour or so.' His thumb did a slow brush over each of her tendons as if he were committing them to memory. He looked at her with a strained gaze. 'I thought I was going to lose you a second time.'

Alice squeezed his hand, her heart giving a little flutter at the depth of caring in his eyes. 'I wish I hadn't left the way I did back then. I ended up hurting myself more than you.'

'We hurt each other, *cara*,' he said. 'I can't believe I was so damn stubborn about it. I could've called you in a day or two. I *should've* called you. But I was too proud. Proud and angry. All those years went by. Not a day passed without me thinking of what could have been.'

His fingers tightened on her hand.

'I thought losing my family was bad, but losing you seven years ago was like a lid slamming down on all of my hopes. I decided it was better to be alone than to invite such rejection again. I've kept every relationship since as shallow and temporary as I could. Until now.'

Until now.

What did that mean? Did it mean he wanted their relationship to continue past the six months laid down in his grandmother's will? Alice reached up to stroke his face.

'We've been such stubborn fools—me in particular. I was so determined not to love anyone in case they took control of me, but I think I fell in love with you that first day when you made me laugh about my backpack catching your clothing. I spent the next six weeks denying it, blocking it. Sabotaging it.'

He pressed his lips against her bent fingers. 'We have a second chance to work at our relationship. Nonna has given us that. But let's talk about that when you're not feeling so out of whack.' He leaned forward to drop a kiss to her forehead. 'I'll sleep in one of the spare rooms so you get a good night's sleep.'

Alice hung onto his hand when he rose from the bed. 'No, don't go.'

'Alice, I—'

'Just hold me, okay?'

He gave a sigh and gathered her close, his chin resting on top of her head. 'As long as you need me I'll be here.'

How about for ever?

CHAPTER ELEVEN

ALICE WOKE THE next morning to find Cristiano lying beside her on top of the bedcovers with his legs crossed at the ankles. He was still fully dressed, although his tie was askew and the first three buttons of his shirt undone and his sleeves rolled up his forearms. His hair was rumpled as if he'd raked his fingers through it and his face looked tired and drawn.

She rolled to her side and tiptoed a fingertip down the bridge of his nose. His face gave a twitch or two and then his eyes opened and he sat bolt upright.

'What?' He sucked in a harsh-sounding breath. 'Oh, sorry, *cara*. You okay? Did you say something?'

'No, I was just watching you sleep.'

He dragged a hand down his face. 'Is that what you call it? I feel like I've been awake for a month.' He narrowed his gaze and lifted his arm to peer at his watch. Dropping it back to the bed with a dead arm flop. 'God. Five a.m.'

Alice stroked her fingers down the raspy slope of his cheek. 'Do you realise that's the first night we've spent together without making love?'

He cranked open one eye. 'Why do you think I'm on the outside of these sheets?'

She nestled closer, leaning over him so her breasts were crushed against his chest. 'I'm not sick now. In fact, I'm fighting fit.'

The other darkly glinting eye opened. 'I thought we weren't supposed to be fighting any more?'

Alice slipped a hand down to where he was as hard as stone. 'Feels to me you're already armed and dangerous.'

He gave her a sexy grin and flipped her so she was lying beneath him, his hand cupping her breast. 'If I were a good man I'd insist you have something to eat and drink before I ravish you.'

She trailed a fingertip across his lower lip. 'I'm only hungry and thirsty for you.'

He took her mouth in a long slow kiss that stirred her senses into overdrive. But just when she thought he'd reach for a condom and take things further, he pulled back and got off the bed. Something about his expression alerted her to a change of mood.

'Sorry, *cara*. I must be a better man than I thought.' He leaned down to brush her forehead with a light-as-air kiss, so light it was just shy of being impersonal. 'Stay right where you are. I'm going to give you breakfast in bed.'

Alice lay back against the pillows while she waited. Maybe they'd talk about their future over breakfast. Surely he hadn't forgotten what he'd said last night?

They'd been given a second chance to work at their relationship.

He was being so kind, so solicitous. He was acting exactly like a man in love…wasn't he? Last night he had looked so distraught at the hospital and again when they'd come home, fussing over her and holding her in his arms all night without getting a wink of sleep him-self. Didn't that mean he loved her?

Then why hadn't he said something?

She'd told him last night she loved him...or at least that she had fallen in love with him the first moment they'd met. Why hadn't he said it back? Or hadn't he said it because he didn't feel that way now? Had his tenderness last night just been a reaction to the shock of finding her in hospital?

Alice couldn't stop the panic rising. What if she'd misread their conversation last night? What if he'd just said those words to settle her for the night after her health scare? Was it her imagination or was he with-drawing from her? When had he ever pulled away from a kiss? Was he backing away from a longer relationship?

Had her confession of love made him rethink their involvement?

In two weeks they would be married, but on what terms? Temporary. No future stretching out in front of them. No plans for making a family together and raising them with love and commitment. Their relationship, al-though it would be formalised with a certificate of mar-riage, would be nothing more than a transient affair—as he'd stated time and time again he wanted it to be.

How could she agree to that when she wanted the opposite?

Yesterday, when the doctor asked Alice if there was any possibility she could be pregnant, a balloon of hope had risen in her chest. But then she'd realised the futil-ity of harbouring such a hope. Cristiano didn't want a family. He didn't want what she wanted.

The sad irony of their reversed wishes made her re-alise again how devastated he must have felt when she'd walked out on him that day in that restaurant. When the pregnancy test came back negative she was both relieved and disappointed. She didn't want to force him to stay with her. She wanted him to love her and commit to her, not because of a baby, not because of his well-meaning grandmother's machinations, but because he loved her more than anything else in the world. More than his stupid old shares, more than a luxury villa.

She thought of her friend Jennifer. She and Cristiano and Jennifer and Marcus would be married within a week of each other and yet you couldn't find two different couples. Jennifer and Marcus were deeply in love. They planned to do all the things young couples on the threshold of a life together planned.

What did Alice and Cristiano have? A six-month time limit. He wanted his shares and his family villa and the only way to get them was to marry her. Without his grandmother's will their affair would not have resumed. She would be fooling herself to think otherwise. He'd had seven years to do something about their 'unfinished business' and he had done nothing.

Cristiano came back with a tray with muesli and toast and juice and tea. One bowl. One plate. One cup. 'Here we go.' He balanced the tray on her knees. 'Breakfast in bed.'

Alice picked up the cup of steaming tea. 'Aren't you going to join me?'

'I have a couple of emails to see to. Stuff to do with the wedding and so on. Do you need a hand choosing a dress? I've got some time today if you're—'

'Don't you know it's bad luck for the groom to see the bride's dress before the wedding?'

Something about his slanted smile made her heart

shrivel like a dried-up leaf. 'It's not like we have to worry about that, do we?'

Alice searched his face for a moment, her teeth worrying her bottom lip. He didn't seem at all fazed by the fact their marriage was going to be temporary. Surely if he cared about her he would say something?

Why wasn't he saying something?

Didn't he have a conscience? Marriage was sacred. No one should enter into it without proper commitment and consent. It was a travesty to do otherwise. Didn't he feel the slightest bit conflicted about what they were doing? There was her answer right there. No. He didn't. All he wanted was the terms of the will ticked off. Goal achieved. Problem solved.

She put her cup back down and lifted the tray off her knees.

'What's wrong?' Cristiano took the tray off her, frowning. 'Why are you getting out of bed?'

Alice got to her feet and pushed her hair back behind her shoulders. 'I'm not sure I can do this.'

'It's just breakfast in bed,' he said. 'No one's insisting you take the day off work, although maybe I should. You push yourself way too hard. Meghan told me you never take a holiday.'

She turned and faced him. 'I thought we were going to talk. So let's talk.'

'About what?'

Alice wrapped her arms around her body as if to contain the emotions threatening to burst out of her. What was with his blank expression? Didn't he remember anything about last night? 'About us. About the fact I love you and want to have a future with you. A family.'

His expression locked down, every muscle on his

face freezing as if turned to marble. 'I don't think now's the right time to talk about—'

'When *is* the right time?' Alice said. 'We have two weeks until we get married. You told me last night we would discuss the fact we've been given a second chance at our relationship via your grandmother. So let's discuss it. I'm not unwell now.'

He moved to the other side of the room, straightening objects on her dressing table that didn't need straightening. His back was turned to her but she could see part of his reflection in the mirror. He was shutting her out. Withdrawing from her.

'Can we talk about this some other time? I have a lot on my mind right now.'

Alice wasn't going to be fobbed off. 'If we don't discuss it now, then I'm afraid I can't marry you. It wouldn't be right for me or for you.'

He turned from the dressing table, a flash of irritation firing off at the back of his gaze and a muscle leaping in his jaw. 'What are you talking about? You stand to inherit millions out of this.'

She let out a frustrated breath. 'Life isn't just about money, Cristiano. It's about much more than that. I don't care about the money. Do you really think if I were motivated by money I would've rejected your proposal seven years ago?'

'We're not talking about back then, Alice.' His voice was deep and steady but that muscle near his mouth was speeding up. 'We're talking about now. I've told you what I'm prepared to commit to and having a family is not even on the whiteboard.'

'I want more than a temporary marriage,' Alice said. 'I want a proper one. I want a family. Last night when the doctor told me I wasn't pregnant I realised how much I wished I were having a baby. But you don't want a baby. You don't want what I want at all.'

His eyes were obsidian black, the tension around his mouth making his lips appear white at the corners. 'We agreed on the terms. You're the one who's been on a soapbox for years about how marriage is a domestic prison for women, and now you want the white picket fence and the double pram?'

Alice held his gaze with a resolve she hadn't thought possible even minutes earlier. But she couldn't back down now. *Wouldn't* back down. He'd had plenty of opportunity to tell her he loved her but he hadn't. Even if he said it now, how could she believe it wasn't a ploy to make her agree to the terms of the will?

'I want the fairy tale and I don't want to settle for anything less than absolute commitment,' she said. 'I want my marriage to be for ever, not for six months.'

He stalked to the other side of the bedroom, his hand rubbing at the back of his neck as if something were burning him there. He swung back to face her, his expression going back to cold, hard marble. 'I'm not going to parrot the words you think you want to hear. Why are you doing this—?'

'I wouldn't believe you if you said you loved me now,' Alice said. 'You're completely focussed on getting those shares and keeping your grandmother's villa in your family's hand. That's all you care about. You don't care about me. I don't think you ever did. You care about what *you* want—what I would do for you by being your wife. Our relationship has always been more about you than us as a unit, and if you were honest with yourself you'd admit it.'

'Alice, listen to me.' His voice softened but she got the sense his anger was not far away. 'You're still not well. You're not thinking straight. You have too much to lose to throw this now. Just hop back into bed and I'll—'

'And you'll what?' Alice cast him a frosty glare. 'Seduce me into seeing things your way? That's what you always tried to do in the past. You never listened to me when we had a difference of opinion. You tried to solve everything with sex. But sex won't solve this. I want more from you than great sex. Much, much more.'

He drew in a deep breath and released it in a whoosh. 'So that's it? Marriage or nothing?'

Alice gave him a wry look. 'Your words, not mine, but they'll do.' She took off her engagement ring and handed it to him. 'I think it's best if we don't see each other again.'

He ignored her outstretched palm, his mouth curling up at one corner. 'Keep it. You can pawn it so you can set up your spa or throw it away for all I care.'

Alice closed her hand around the ring, not one bit surprised when it cut into her palm as sharply as his words had into her heart. 'You won't ever be happy, Cristiano, because deep down you don't think you deserve to be. You refuse to love someone in case they withdraw that love or fate takes it away from you.'

He snatched up his jacket from the back of the dressing-table chair. 'Leave your psychoanalysis for someone who gives a damn. You don't know me as well as you think.'

'I know,' Alice said. 'That's why we were doomed from the start. You don't want anyone to get close to you. I can't be in a relationship like that. I want emotional honesty.' *I want you to love me.*

'Oh, and you're the big expert on emotional honesty, aren't you, Alice?' His eyes blazed with bitterness. 'You think I'm going to believe you're suddenly madly in love with me? A few days ago you wanted to gouge my eyes out. What you're doing is manipulating. Trying to get your future sorted by issuing me with an ultimatum. How about a bit of intellectual honesty, hey? Let's try that instead. I can't give you what you want. Simple as that. Take it or leave it.'

'I don't hate you. I never hated you.'

He gave a snort. 'Yeah, well, guess what? I don't give a damn either way.'

Alice winced when the bedroom door snapped shut on his exit. She listened to the tread of his footsteps as he left her house, her breath stalling in the hope he would stop and turn back. Come back up the stairs and swing open her bedroom door and say he was sorry. That he would sweep her into his arms and say of course he loved her and wanted to spend the rest of his life with her.

But the only thing she got was silence.

Cristiano had never felt so flooded with such confusing emotions. Anger. Disappointment. Bitterness. Anger again. A hot cauldron of bubbling feelings was threatening to explode out of his chest. He had to stop to lean over and place his hands on his knees to get control of his breath. In. Out. In. Out. How could she do this to him? Now?

Two weeks.

Two miserable weeks and his shares and the villa would have been secure.

Why? Why? Why?

He'd thought they were fine. He'd thought everything was ticking along just as he'd wanted it. But just like seven years ago she had blindsided him. His guard had been down. He was so thrown by her being taken to hospital he hadn't seen what was right in front of him. That sexy little crawl over his chest to make him feel secure and then *wham*! She wanted to control him. Manipulate him into doing things her way.

No way was he going to be her puppet. He'd told her the terms. He'd been honest about what he was prepared to give. She was the one shifting the goalposts.

Just like you did in the past, dropping that proposal on her.

Cristiano swatted away the thought as if it were an annoying fly. *So?* He'd shifted them right on back. A short-term marriage was all he was prepared to have. And even that was a stretch. He didn't want the responsibility of maintaining a long-term relationship. He didn't want the *emotional honesty* such a relationship demanded.

If he opened up the vault of his heart then that would undo all the work he'd put in since he was that boy of eleven hearing his parents and brother were never coming back. He could not allow himself to be that vulnerable. Not again. Look at what last night had done to him. Rushing into that hospital to see Alice had thrown him into a chest-seizing panic. He'd lain awake most of the night with residual dread still chugging through his veins like jagged cubes of ice. He hadn't trusted her confession of love last night. If she'd loved him way back then, why had she walked out and never looked back?

You did the same to her.

Cristiano didn't want to be reminded of how badly he'd handled things in the past. It was better this way. He couldn't give her what she wanted. He wasn't that person any more. Maybe he'd never been that person. He was too damaged by the loss of his family. He kept people at a distance. He controlled them because it was the only way he could harness the fear. The fear that clawed at him. The fear that reminded him with sharp little jabs of how easily he could lose the ones he dared to love. It was easier not to love. To not even think about the word. To pretend his feelings were something else. Lust, attraction, mild affection.

Anything but love.

By the time Alice got to work she had another headache. But the pain in her head was nothing to the pain in her heart. Cristiano had summed up his feelings about her. He didn't give a damn either way. He could take her or leave her. He had chosen to leave her.

'Hey, where's your engagement ring?' Meghan asked when she came in for the day. 'My first client wants to see it. She read about you and Cristiano on...' She frowned. 'Is something wrong?'

Alice blinked away the moisture in her eyes. 'Cristiano and I are not getting married after all. We've broken—'

'Not getting married?' Meghan gasped. 'Why the hell not? You two are the most in love couple I've ever seen. The air crackles like a power station when you guys are in the same room.'

Alice pressed her lips together to stop them from trembling. 'He doesn't love me. He's...oh, it's too complicated to explain.'

'What do you mean he doesn't love you?' Meghan's eyes were slit-thin with incredulity. 'You should've seen him when he came here yesterday and found out you were in hospital. I thought he was going to pass out on the spot. He was as white as our deluxe collagen face mask.'

Alice wished it were true. Wished he loved her. But if he loved her he wouldn't be baulking at commitment. That was what love was all about. Commitment. Trust. A future, not a time line.

'He doesn't want what I want. He doesn't want kids.'

Meghan's face fell. 'Oh…well then, that's a deal-breaker.' But then she brightened again. 'But maybe he'll change his mind. Lots of men do. They come round to it eventually, when they—'

'He won't,' Alice said. 'He's stubborn like that.'

Meghan waggled her eyebrows. 'Mmm, like some-one else I know.'

Alice frowned. 'Don't you have work to do?'

Meghan gave her a 'kicked puppy' look. 'I'm really sorry about you breaking up with Cristiano. But he's had a lot going on in his life—his gran dying and this big new development. Maybe he needs a bit of time to think things over.'

'Like another seven years?'

Meghan bit her lip. 'He really is stubborn, isn't he?'

Alice gave her a grim look. 'He could open a men-toring academy for mules.'

CHAPTER TWELVE

CRISTIANO WAS PRESSING on with his London development on principle. He wasn't the sort of man to walk away from a business deal because of personal issues. He kept work and his private life separate. Mostly. Although having to visit the Chelsea site with Alice's beauty salon on the ground floor of the building he'd bought was like having molars pulled with bolt cutters. Confronting failure was something he assiduously avoided. Returning to the scene of the crime, so to speak, was anathema to him. He would prefer to be on the other side of the globe right now. Siberia. Outer Mongolia.

Anywhere but here.

Somehow the press had heard the engagement was off. He had refused to comment and apparently so had Alice as the articles were evidently from 'reliable sources close to the couple' whatever the hell that meant. But after a week of being chased to and from his hotel by the paparazzi, things had settled down.

Seven days of living without Alice. Not seeing her. Not touching her. Not making love to her.

Nothing.

A big yawning cavern of emptiness stretched out ahead of him. Just like the last time, only this time it was harder. Much harder. How had he done this before and for seven years? He'd convinced himself he'd done the right thing. Let her be free to live the life he couldn't give her. But the thought of her getting on with her life without him was eating away at him. Gnawing on his nerves until he was all but twitching with restlessness.

Cristiano had to meet with the architect on site to discuss some of the plans he had for the refit of the building. But the whole time he was in the meeting his eyes kept drifting to the window in the hope of seeing Alice coming in or out of her salon.

He was surprised the architect didn't notice, or maybe he did and was too polite to say anything. He'd noticed a wedding ring on the architect's finger and noticed too the screensaver on the guy's phone when he answered a call. It was a photo of his wife and young toddler and newborn baby. All the things Cristiano had convinced himself he didn't want.

But he *did* want them.

The realisation was like a light being switched on, shining on all the dark lonely places in his heart. Illuminating the hopes and dreams he had stashed and hidden away out of fear.

Cristiano finished the meeting and was about to turn left away from Alice's salon when he stopped mid-stride. This was ridiculous. What was he doing? Walking away a second time? Turning his back on the best thing that had ever happened to him? Who was he fooling?

He wasn't in lust with Alice. He was in love. He had always been in love with her. That was why he was so damn terrified. That was why he'd rushed the proposal seven years ago. He'd been so worried he might lose her so he'd made her an offer he'd thought she wouldn't be able to refuse.

But he'd got it all wrong. So horribly wrong.

He'd thought losing the shares and his *nonna*'s villa was the worst thing that could happen to him. But losing Alice was far worse. He couldn't lose her. Not again.

He had to talk to her. He couldn't let another day— another minute—pass without telling her he loved her and wanted the same things she wanted. Why had he left it a week? Seven days of miserable hell. No way was he leaving it a second longer.

He spun on his heel and went back the other way but he'd only taken two strides when he saw Meghan from Alice's beauty salon trotting towards him.

'Hi, Cristiano,' she said. 'Bad news about your breakup with Alice. But don't worry. I've got it all sorted. I've found her a new man. I'm setting up a blind date for her. He's a friend of a friend and he's so keen on having kids he's already got cupboards full of toys. Isn't that sweet?'

Cristiano felt as if he'd been slammed across the head with a plank. 'A blind date?'

'Yup.' Meghan's eyes twinkled. 'It worked a treat for one of our clients. They're getting married this weekend. Jennifer and Marcus. Alice is doing Jennifer's make-up for it.'

Cristiano had trouble speaking past the knot of despair stuck in his throat. 'She can't do that.'

'What?' Meghan's expression was guileless as a child. 'Do Jennifer's make-up? Don't be silly. That's her specialty!'

What Alice's specialty was to make him as mad as a wasp-stung bull. How could she date another man so quickly? What the hell was she doing going on a blind date? What if the guy was a freak? Some stranger who would— He couldn't bear to think about it. Jealousy rose in him like bile. He was choking on it. He could feel it bubbling up his windpipe like an overflowing drain. 'Where is she?' he asked.

Meghan pointed to the salon. 'She's in her office working on accounts. But she doesn't want to be—'

'You can cancel your friend of a friend, okay?' Cristiano said. 'If she's going on a date with anyone it's going to be with me.'

Alice couldn't concentrate on the rows of numbers on her computer screen. Normally seeing all those healthy figures would have made her do a happy dance. But she had never felt more miserable. A week had gone past and no word from Cristiano. Not even a text message. Nothing. A big fat nothing. The press had done their thing for a few days but she'd refused to speak to them. She'd even resorted to using disguises to avoid them when walking to and from her house or the salon.

Her mother had been 'too upset' to talk to her, which was typical. As if it was Alice's fault the marriage wasn't going ahead. Well, it was, but that was beside the point. But how could she go ahead with a marriage that was the opposite of what a marriage should be? What she wanted *her* marriage to be?

Meghan had been a stalwart support, making numerous cups of tea and bringing in a steady supply of cinnamon-covered doughnuts—Alice's weakness when dealing with stress. Sugar and fat were the only pleasures she had in her life now.

There was the sound of bell tinkling as the salon door

opened…although tinkling wasn't the right word. Firm footsteps came striding through the salon and Alice barely had time to get to her feet when her office door slammed back against the wall and Cristiano appeared. 'What the hell do you think you're doing?'

Alice kept her expression cool and composed even though her heart rate was doing its hummingbird impersonation. 'Accounts. It's been a good week for me. One of my best, actually.'

His expression was thunderous, all stormy clouds and dark shadows and lightning flashes in his eyes. 'Meghan tells me you're dating someone else.'

Alice frowned. 'What?'

His mouth was pressed into a chalk-white line. 'Don't do it, Alice.' He released a tight breath. 'Please.'

Alice was starting to join some dots and it was creating an interesting picture indeed. 'When were you speaking to Meghan?'

'Just now, outside.' He jerked his head towards the street. 'She said she was setting you up on a blind date with some friend of a friend who wants kids.'

'I don't know anything about a blind date,' Alice said. 'And you've got a hide storming in here telling me what to do with my private life when it's no concern of yours and nor will it ever—'

'If you want to have kids so badly then you can damn well have them with me.'

Alice opened her mouth to fling back another round of fire but stopped and gaped at him instead. Had she heard him correctly? Kids? He wanted kids? But then she realised what was going on. Jealousy. Not love. The big green-eyed monster was behind his change of heart.

She narrowed her gaze. 'So, let me get this straight. .

You're offering to be a sperm donor and a cardboard cut-out husband because you're...*jealous*?' She said the word as if it were some sort of contagion.

Cristiano came around to her side of the desk and grasped her by the upper arms.

'Damn straight I am. Alice, I love you. I've been a stubborn fool all this time refusing to acknowledge it. I can handle the loss of the shares. I can handle the loss of the villa. What I can't handle is the loss of you. I've already lost you once. I don't want to lose you again. I was already coming here when I ran into Meghan. Please believe me, *cara*. Don't let anything else keep us apart. Will you marry me? Not because of Nonna's will, not because I'm jealous but because I love you and want to spend the rest of my life with you.'

Alice looked at him with watering eyes. 'Do you mean it? You're not just saying it because of the deadline?'

His hold tightened as if he were terrified she was going to slip out of his grasp. 'I don't care about the deadline other than I want to do what Nonna wanted. She knew I hadn't got over you. She knew I was too stubborn to see you again so she orchestrated it so I had no choice.'

Alice smiled. 'Like Meghan.'

He frowned. 'Meghan?'

Alice laced her arms around his neck. 'I'm not going on a blind date. Why would I do that when I only have eyes for you?'

Relief washed over his features and he smiled. 'The little meddling minx. She and Nonna must be kindred spirits.' He gathered her tight against his body. 'She saw what Nonna saw, what I refused to see. I love you, *tesoro mio*. I love you desperately. Please say you'll marry me.'

Alice looked into his handsome features so full of love and adoration for her. The softness in his dark brown eyes, the way he looked at her as if she were the most precious thing he could ever hold in his arms— made her feel so happy she could barely speak.

'I will marry you, darling. I can't think of anything I would rather do than be your wife and the mother of your children.'

He crushed her mouth beneath his in a kiss that spoke of the depth of his feelings. He drew back to smile at her, his own eyes suspiciously moist.

'I've spent so much of my life avoiding getting close to people in case I lost them. But I got to thinking I might as well have jumped in my family's coffins with them if I don't live a full and authentic life. I owe it to them to make the most of the time that was snatched away from them.'

Alice touched the track of dampness leaking from his eyes. 'I wish I'd been able to meet them. I'm sure they were wonderful people who loved you so much. They would be thrilled you're embracing life at last. I'm sure of it.'

Cristiano brushed her hair back with his hand. 'I've been thinking about what we can do together. You could have your wedding spa as a feature of my hotel. Here in London but also in Italy and France and Greece. You could have your own franchise. It will be something to build together.'

Alice held his face in her hands and kissed him. 'You are making all my dreams come true. I would love that.

It would be so wonderful to do it together just like your grandparents and parents did.'

He kissed her soundly, only breaking away to gaze down at her with a look of such devotion it made Alice's eyes tear up again.

'We've only got a week to pull off this wedding,' he said. 'Do you think we can do it?'

She stroked his lean jaw, and looked lovingly into his eyes. 'Together we can do anything.'

One year later...

Alice smiled at Cristiano as he came in from bringing in their bags from the car. They were spending their first wedding anniversary at his grandmother's villa where they came every few months to relax and recharge. Yes, *relax*. That word she used not to have in her vocabulary.

Her beauty spa at Cristiano's Chelsea hotel had finally opened a few weeks ago to great fanfare and she had recently appointed Meghan as her business manager and it was working a treat. It meant Alice could have the occasional week off without worrying about her clients not receiving the attention she prided herself on giving them.

And because she intended to take even more time off in a few months' time.

Alice took Cristiano by the hand and led him to the walnut table in the sitting room where the family photos were arranged. Whenever they came back to the villa they stood there and quietly acknowledged his family. Their wedding photo was next to his parents' and grandparents' wedding photos, creating a sense of continuity she knew gave him great comfort. It gave her great comfort too to see him so happy and settled after so much heartache. She hadn't told him yet, but soon there would be photos of the next generation of the Marchetti family.

'I have something to tell you, darling,' Alice said, squeezing his hand in excitement. 'I wanted to wait until we got here so the rest of the family could hear it as well.'

Cristiano's dark brown eyes misted. 'You're... *pregnant*?'

'I did a test this morning. I've been bursting to tell you but then I thought how lovely it would be for you to hear about it here amongst those who loved you so deeply.'

He gathered her close, kissing her tenderly and then holding her with such gentleness she had trouble keeping her own tears in check.

'How far along?' he said. 'Are you okay? Not sick? Feeling faint? Shouldn't you be resting? What about work—?'

Alice put a fingertip to his mouth to stall his speech. 'Meghan is going to cover me while I take maternity leave. And I feel fantastic...well, apart from a tiny bit of squeamishness. I'm six weeks pregnant according to my calculations. It must have been the weekend of the opening of your hotel and my spa.' She gave him a twinkling look. 'I seem to remember we had a lot of fun together that weekend.'

Cristiano cupped her face in his hands, his own eyes gleaming. 'I didn't know the meaning of the word until I met you. You've made me so happy, *cara*.'

Alice smiled and drew his head back down so her lips were within reach of his. 'We make each other happy, which is what your *nonna* recognised right from the start. I can't imagine how miserable I would be now if it hadn't been for her meddling.'

Cristiano grinned. 'Wise woman, my *nonna*. She knew there was only one woman in the world for me.'

He brushed her mouth with his. Once. Twice. Three times.

'You.'

* * * * *

If you enjoyed this story, don't miss these other great reads from Melanie Milburne

UNWRAPPING HIS CONVENIENT FIANCÉE
HIS MISTRESS FOR A WEEK
THE MOST SCANDALOUS RAVENSDALE
ENGAGED TO HER RAVENSDALE ENEMY
AWAKENING THE RAVENSDALE HEIRESS
RAVENSDALE'S DEFIANT CAPTIVE

Available now!

MILLS & BOON®

EXCLUSIVE EXTRACT

Stefano Moretti wants only revenge from his wife, Anna. When she reappears after leaving him, with no memory of their marriage, he realizes that this is his chance…for a red-hot private seduction, followed by a public humiliation! Until Stefano realizes there's something he wants more than vengeance—Anna, back in his bed for good!

Read on for a sneak preview of
ONCE A MORETTI WIFE

Stefano pressed his thumb to her chin and gently stroked it. 'When your memories come back you will know the truth. I will help you find them.'

Her heart thudding, her skin alive with the sensation of his touch, Anna swallowed the moisture that had filled her mouth.

When had she given in to the chemistry that had always been there between them, always pulling her to him? She'd fought against it right from the beginning, having no intention of joining the throng of women Stefano enjoyed such a legendary sex life with. To be fair, she didn't have any evidence of what he actually got up to under the bedsheets; indeed it was something she'd been resolute in *not* thinking about, but the steady flow of glamorous, sexy women in and out of his life had been pretty damning.

When had she gone from liking and hugely admiring

him but with an absolute determination to never get into bed with him, to marrying him overnight? She'd heard of whirlwind marriages before but from employee to wife in twenty-four hours? Her head hurt just trying to wrap itself around it.

Had Stefano looked at her with the same glimmer in his green eyes then as he was now? Had he pressed his lips to hers or had she been the one...?

'How will you help me remember us?' she asked in a whisper.

His thumb moved to caress her cheek and his voice dropped to a murmur. 'I will help you find again the pleasure you had in my bed. I will teach you to become a woman again.'

Mortification suffused her, every part of her anatomy turning red.

I will teach you to be a woman again?

His meaning was clear. He knew she was a virgin.

Anna's virginity was not something she'd ever discussed with anyone. Why would she? Twenty-three-year-old virgins were rarer than the lesser-spotted unicorn. For Stefano to know that...

Dear God, it was *true*.

All the denial she'd been storing up fell away.

She really had married him.

Don't miss
ONCE A MORETTI WIFE
By Michelle Smart

Available April 2017
www.millsandboon.co.uk

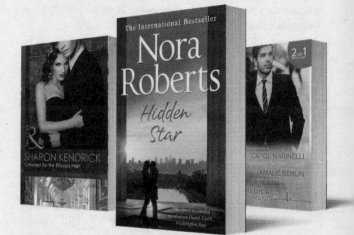

MILLS & BOON®

Congratulations
Carol Marinelli
on your 100th Mills & Boon book!

Read on for an exclusive extract

How did she walk away? Lydia wondered.

How did she go over and kiss that sulky mouth and say goodbye when really she wanted to climb back into bed?

But rather than reveal her thoughts she flicked that internal default switch which had been permanently set to 'polite'.

'Thank you so much for last night.'

'I haven't finished being your tour guide yet.'

He stretched out his arm and held out his hand but Lydia didn't go over. She did not want to let in hope, so she just stood there as Raul spoke.

'It would be remiss of me to let you go home without seeing Venice as it should be seen.'

'Venice?'

'I'm heading there today. Why don't you come with me? Fly home tomorrow instead.'

There was another night between now and then, and Lydia knew that even while he offered her an extension he made it clear there was a cut-off.

Time added on for good behaviour.

And Raul's version of 'good behaviour' was that there would

be no tears or drama as she walked away. Lydia knew that. If she were to accept his offer then she had to remember that.

'I'd like that.' The calm of her voice belied the trembling she felt inside. 'It sounds wonderful.'

'Only if you're sure?' Raul added.

'Of course.'

But how could she be sure of anything now she had set foot in Raul's world?

He made her dizzy.

Disorientated.

Not just her head, but every cell in her body seemed to be spinning as he hauled himself from the bed and unlike Lydia, with her sheet-covered dash to the bathroom, his body was hers to view.

And that blasted default switch was stuck, because Lydia did the right thing and averted her eyes.

Yet he didn't walk past. Instead Raul walked right over to her and stood in front of her.

She could feel the heat—not just from his naked body but her own—and it felt as if her dress might disintegrate.

He put his fingers on her chin, tilted her head so that she met his eyes, and it killed that he did not kiss her, nor drag her back to his bed. Instead he checked again. 'Are you sure?'

'Of course,' Lydia said, and tried to make light of it. 'I never say no to a free trip.'

It was a joke but it put her in an unflattering light. She was about to correct herself, to say that it hadn't come out as she had meant, but then she saw his slight smile and it spelt approval.

A gold-digger he could handle, Lydia realised.

Her emerging feelings for him—perhaps not.

At every turn her world changed, and she fought for a semblance of control. Fought to convince not just Raul but herself that she could handle this.

Don't miss
THE INNOCENT'S SECRET BABY
by Carol Marinelli
OUT NOW

BUY YOUR COPY TODAY
www.millsandboon.co.uk

Join Britain's BIGGEST Romance Book Club

50% OFF your first parcel

- **EXCLUSIVE offers every month**
- **FREE delivery direct to your door**
- **NEVER MISS a title**
- **EARN Bonus Book points**

Call Customer Services
0844 844 1358*

or visit
millsandboon.co.uk/subscriptions

* This call will cost you 7 pence per minute plus your phone company's price per minute access charge.